# MY HAUNTED JOURNEY

BRADFORD SCOTT

# <u>DISCLAIMER</u>

Some of these locations I have been to only once due to various circumstances; like them being torn down or no longer being accessible. As such so some chapters may be a bit shorter when it comes to the paranormal stuff, but I don't want any trip, or any location to go unnoticed, unused and wasted. I ***do not*** condone or recommend what I do for this. I do it to preserve history and share the stories of any spirits who may be stuck at the locations and want to share their story. ***It is not safe by any means, so do not attempt to recreate my actions yourself***. A few of them are now state parks and you can roam the grounds during posted hours, just do your research first before going to any of the places.

# DEDICATION

This book is dedicated to both of my amazing children, Braiden and Jacksen. Both of them are a big part of why I still do this. They always want to see my adventures, hear the stories and are my biggest fans. Especially Jacksen. They kept me going, when I almost gave up. My mother-in-law, Diana, for buying me all those Urbex and haunted location books. Helping me find new places for me to explore myself. Feeding the addiction. To all the spirits stuck in these locations, that had to live a life that they did. May their souls find peace they deserve.

# THANK YOU

I wanted to give a quick thank you to all of those who have been cheering me on since I started this adventure. The ones who are always rooting for me. Thank you to those of you who are crazy enough to go with me to some of these locations so I can do what I do. You know who you are. I have met a lot of awesome explorers along my years of doing this, and I am thankful for each and one of you.

# TABLE OF CONTENT

# PROLOGUE

Are you ready to safely step into some abandoned locations with some disturbing pasts? Are you ready to hear some chilling paranormal encounters at each one? Some paranormal moments that are simply mind blowing? Well, dim the lights, grab your favorite reading snack, and let's dive into some locations that are both beautiful yet creepy. Each chapter will be about a different location and contain real paranormal experiences as well as a brief history of each location.

I know the risks I take when going to some of these locations and do not recommend replicating my actions. I will try to keep each chapter short, sweet, and right to the point without missing too much. Have you ever been ghost hunting? Been curious about what it is really like? I will tell you now, it's not what you have seen on television. That is why I started this journey, watching all those shows, something just didn't seem right. And it was the fact that they make the unknown seem scarier than what it really is.

Don't get me wrong, I have been in some scary ass situations but that is because I put myself in them. Like going to some of these abandoned hospitals where many people have passed away ALONE! Or in small groups of 2-3 people at most. But I've always walked away unharmed. Well, except for one location. A spirit followed me home. Even in some of the scarier locations with some darker energy, do you know what the most common phrases I have come across while speaking to the other side are?

"Help me."

"Save us."

"Help us."

Help them with what? Save them from what? They have already passed away; there is nothing left to fear, right? Nothing left to do, right? Wrong. Some of them want to be heard, want their stories to be shared. Just have someone to talk to them again. They are trapped in these locations for various reasons. Waiting for someone like me to come along. Someone willing to hear their story.

And that's where almost all television shows go wrong. Most of them fabricate stories to make these places seem scarier, all the spirits seem evil. Because let's be real, the most important thing is ratings, right? Welcome to a world consumed by greed. Even in the afterlife greed casts a shadow over all of us. Well, now is the time to let the light shine over the darkness, we, as humans have cast over the voiceless. Over ourselves, both alive and on the other side.

I am not saying there is no such thing as bad spirits. That is like saying there are no bad people. We have the good, we have the bad. Ying and yang. But this book, this story, however you want to label it, is for those who want real stories, real paranormal experiences. No ratings, no critics. Just a person sharing the good, the bad, the beautiful, and the ugly with no one influencing how this journey goes. Well, except for those beyond the grave.

So, without further ado, let's take a trip to really amazing locations, learn some history about each one of them, and share some crazy paranormal moments that I personally lived through at each one.

Welcome to;

My Haunted Journey- Part One: True Paranormal Encounters in Abandoned Places.

# CHAPTER 1:

## SALTWATER THERAPY

Okay, now that I have wasted enough time with that opening, let's get this journey started with one of my personal favorites, SEASIDE SANITARIUM. Located in Waterford, CT, this shell of a hospital as old and decaying as it is, is an absolute beauty of older architecture. It was designed by Cass Gilbert, who also helped design the Woolworth building in New York City, as well as Union Station in New Haven. It was originally built as a tuberculosis hospital for children in the 1930's and Cass incorporated that into the design. It was designed to allow ample sunlight, and the fresh saltwater air was thought to be therapeutic and help the children with the disease.

The Maher building, one of the few buildings still remaining, (at the time of writing this, it is in the works of possible demolition) is the building that caught the most sunlight with its open terraces and places for

patients to sunbathe. The hospital also had a school, dormitories, and a cafeteria. Children received lessons, enjoyed music, practiced sports, but most of all, they were able to enjoy the ocean front beach. It is said most children would spend six to twelve months there, some less than that.

Fast forward to the late 1940's when medicine to cure tuberculosis had been devised, heliotropic treatment was no longer practiced, so this hospital like other tuberculosis hospitals, shut down. Not letting the building and grounds go to waste it reopened its doors in 1958 for a whole 3 years as an elderly home by the name Seaside Geriatric Hospital. That brings us to 1961 when the hospital is repurposed once again as a mental facility known as Seaside Regional Center for the mentally retarded. Claims of poor management, patient abuse, and a high death toll, the establishment was forced to close its doors for good in 1996. Between its opening days for tuberculosis and its closing days as an institution the death toll hasn't been fully confirmed but is estimated to be in the low hundreds.

Now a state park with an amazing view, people are always going to the beach to relax, sunbathe, walk their dog, and just enjoy the peacefulness of the land that masks the past of what once was. At the time of me writing this, like I mentioned, the Maher building still stands as well as a little wooden bridge that passes over a little creek and the administration building. The

grounds are open to the public from sunrise to sunset; however, the buildings are fenced off and people are discouraged from entering them. There are back and forth cases with the state between trying to demolish what remains and cases trying to save the buildings for historical purposes. There was another hearing at the end of Summer/Fall of 2024 of what would happen with these buildings. As of right now, it is still in the development phase. They will tear down what is left of the buildings eventually and make a park.

Now that I have given a quick history lesson of this location let's dive into the juicy stuff, the spooky stuff. Why I keep going back to this location and why it is one of my personal favorites. My journey of dabbling in the paranormal started in September of 2019 and this was one of the first locations I really got my feet wet with. I was tired of watching the "shows" and hearing their prattle on how EVERYTHING is "*evil*" and wanted to set out for myself, to see for myself what it really is like. And Seaside was that icebreaker.

I can still remember the first time I stepped foot on those grounds like it was just yesterday, the first time I saw those massive and beautiful buildings and how amazing that ocean front view is. Remember how I mentioned claims of "poor" management and the institution being on the chaotic side? Well, as I was walking the perimeter setting up cameras to sit and record the windows on the backside of the hospital, you know, in case a spirit wanted to walk by, a woman was passing by walking her dog. She was local to the area and asked what I was doing and I was honest with her. I told her we were "ghost hunting."

That is when she told me how she was a child when the institution was open and she was in the girl scouts. She mentioned how in good faith they thought it would be a good idea to bring them some cookies. She said her and her fellow scout members were at the main door and as soon as they opened up that big main door, they could hear people screaming like crazy, screaming in pain, and watched people running around like it was a zoo. She said it was a terrifying sight; it scared them all off and they never returned. It was amazing to have come across that lady and hear that story. Unfortunately, I didn't catch her name, and if you come across this and read this, "*Thank you.*"

I mentioned I have been coming to this site for a couple years now, so I have plenty of moments to share with you all but let's talk about the ones I will never forget. Back to trip one, three memorable moments happened this day. It was an overcast day, barely anyone there other than a few people passing through walking their dogs, like that lady who told me that story. Well, remember how I said I mentioned I staged a couple cameras? It definitely paid off. I didn't capture any apparitions in the window like I was hoping but caught a residual EVP (electronic voice phenomenon) and poltergeist like activity. The EVP was of a little boy calling out for his mom. Was this a child who was stuck here during the tuberculosis hospital time? Was he one of the few who unfortunately didn't make it? I hope one day to find out, but that EVP is so clear, there was no mistaking what was said. Sounds residual (a moment stuck in time) and I wonder if I will ever be able to make contact with that child.

The second moment was the other camera that was staged recording the opposite side of the back end of the hospital is the one that received poltergeist like activity. It is a $1500 camera that was on a tripod. I was NOT letting that thing leave my sight. I would walk up and down the side of the hospital or along the back side but no matter where I was, that camera was still in my vision. Well, somehow, some way, someone who was NOT there with me poked at my camera. As I was watching the footage I noticed it sounds like someone tap my camera and as it gets tapped, you see the frame shake. This was not wind; this was not a fluke. The camera goes from perfectly still to the quick shake with the tap noises back to perfectly still. That moment still baffles me. Who was so curious about my camera that they poked at it?

Moment three is pretty crazy too. Myself, and the person I was with were staging up on the side where the main door is. We were setting up on this concrete pillar, it resembles the remnants of what would have been some kind of statue or a little waterfall display, something to make the place look more elegant. It is falling apart now, so kind of hard to tell exactly what it is. Well, we had staged a voice recorder on it and as we were getting our video cameras ready for footage you can hear an EVP of a man say, "watch this, they are going to record." That is an intelligent EVP, meaning that spirit was there with us, and knew exactly what we were up too. An EVP that I will never forget.

This was all during the first visit there! Now I needed more, this place had me hooked. So, we went back for trip number two. This one, as it happens was more on the chill, quiet side. It happens. Ghost hunting is a lot like fishing. You may catch a lovely big fish, you may catch a little pumpkinhead (kiver), or you may catch nothing at all. But when a spirit calls you out by name, and you're not use to that, well that will catch you off guard and mess with your head, and that's exactly what happened.

I was walking over to the administration building which is a good twenty or more feet away from the little wooden covered bridge with my K2 meter. This reads EMF (Electronic Magnetic Fluctuation), basically spikes of energy. And as I got closer to the building it started to light up, meaning there were pulses of energy around. I had my phone on airplane mode; there is no power to the buildings and the person I was with was still about thirty feet or more behind me. So, I am wondering why the rise in energy. As I stood there I asked if someone was there, if anyone was around and as I was talking, crystal clear, I heard someone call my name, "Brad." A disembodied voice, where you hear a spirit without any tools, with your own ears.

This is nothing scary, but being newer to this at the time, it honestly caught me off guard and gave me a quick startle. I paused for a quick moment to wrap my head around what had just happened. I even turned to the other person who is now down by the wooden bridge to see if it was him, he said no, and I asked him again to make sure, and he still said no and he said he heard what he thought was a little kid. And I could barely hear him being down by that bridge, yet that voice calling my name was as clear as if they were standing right next to me. A moment I would never be able to forget, even if I wanted to. But why me? Why were they calling me out by name? Answers I will probably never get, especially because this wasn't the last time this happened here.

Trip number three, oh boy. This one, this one is a classic! I was with a different crowd, and we went more on the sneaky side. We were going to take advantage of some holes in the fence and make the trip worth it. Mostly went for pictures and to get to see the inside of these glorious buildings, but I can't just go for pictures, I want the spooky stuff. We were walking towards the end of the hall on the side of the building that has something like a big farmer's porch on it. Again, I had the K2 meter out and it was nice and dark. Well, as I hit the porch like area the K2 meter went crazy and at the time, that was all we saw.

At home, as I was reviewing the footage to get it ready to publish on YouTube, that's when I saw what was really caught, AN APPARITION! That's right, I caught a spirit on video! What makes this even crazier is it happened right in front of our faces and none of us had a clue at the time. The way the spirit moved elegantly, just quickly flowing right by us. There are rumors of a nurse who haunts this building and I strongly believe it was her. Remember how I mentioned them calling me out by name wasn't the last time it was going to happen, well that's because it happened again during that trip. I didn't hear it nice and clear as a disembodied voice this time, but as an EVP. We were in the staircase and once again someone was trying to get my attention from the other side. The clip of the apparition was featured on a television show, Fright Club, with another spirit I caught on video, but that's another location for another chapter.

Are you starting to see why I like this place so much? Every time I go it is an amazing, unforgettable experience. Let's go over trip number four, where I get

a little more on the crazier side. I have seen what this place was capable of and at this point I really want to push the connection and adrenaline rush. I go, and I enter the administration and hospital building ALONE! By golly this trip pushed my nerves to the limit. It was a damp, rainy day which sometimes seems to amplify the energy of locations. And the storm definitely charged this place up!

Being in a few other locations that were "bigger" and "scarier" I thought this would be a walk in the park. But the second I hopped through that basement window and was standing in the middle of a pitch-black basement I could feel all the attention focused on me. You know that feeling that you're not alone, even though you physically may be? That is because our bodies can sense the energy. Now imagine that feeling to the point in which you feel surrounded, almost suffocated by being crowded so badly. To the point you're frozen stiff not knowing what to do. That was me, in that moment. I quickly turned my phone light on so I could grab my real flashlight as I tried to keep my composure and stop myself from leaving right back out that window faster than I went in.

I got my flashlight on and quickly headed for the middle of the building where the stairs are located so I could get the hell out of that dark, creepy basement and get to a floor that had at least some light for comfort. Once I regained my composure, settled down my racing mind, I headed right for where I had caught that spirit on video. I knew I wasn't going to get lucky enough to have it happen again, I wanted to try and at least make contact with the spirit, try to find out who my mystery apparition was. I ran a few EVP sessions, used my modified radio to try and talk but no such luck. I kept hearing "people" walk around me; phantom footsteps. But I could see I wasn't getting any answers, so I left. To be honest with all the energy my body was picking up on, I didn't have any patience either. I wanted to get out of there. I felt like I was "pushing my luck" being in there. So, I thanked the spirits that did chat for that brief moment and got the hell out of there. I was in there maybe an hour tops.

I made my way out and headed over to the main hospital (Maher) building. I thought if the administration building was that charged up, the big guy should be too. I was wrong, dead wrong. I even walked my way down to the basement, and NOTHING! It felt so eerily quiet, perfectly still that I just walked around and took some pictures. I tried a couple EVP sessions with no luck. I knew I wasn't tempting and pushing my luck with the admin building again and this one was going nowhere so, I packed up and called that trip done.

Fast forward to 2024. I have read online about the works of demolishing the buildings. So, I know time is running low of visiting this place and having those beautiful buildings still standing. Don't get me wrong, I know the grounds are 100% haunted and the buildings don't mean anything. There's something about those couple of structures that I can't put into words. Anyways, I am now at the point where I want to push my intuitive side more, the ability to communicate with spirits without any tools and I knew this would be a good practice spot. So, I grabbed my headphones, a notebook, and pen and made my way to Seaside.

I got to the location and set up a chair over by a tree that is about thirty feet from the admin building. I threw on some meditation music with one of my phones and SpiritTalker on another. SpiritTalker is a communication application, hands down the best ones you can use. Nothing comes close to how scary accurate this one is. Created by an engineer that goes by Spotted Ghosts. It is available on iOS and Android for a one-time purchase. Once I was set up and ready to go, I closed my eyes and wrote down whatever the spirits relayed to me via telepathy. This trip was far from being a "spooky" visit yet, this was one of my favorites with Seaside.

One of the spirits who strongly made their presence known was that of a child. He was a Caucasian boy with brown hair that was medium length. He was about eight years old when he got sick. What kept him strong and going was the hopes of seeing his mom again. He was there for about six months before passing away. He really enjoyed drawing, coloring, and playing with his toy dinosaurs.

Another spirit who strongly came through, was that of a nurse. She was about thirty-five years old. Dark haired, well liked, and pretty. She worked there during the asylum days. She really enjoyed working there because she liked trying to help others because she was battling her own demons, which she hid very well. She loved piano music and older jazz type music. When she had the spare time, she enjoyed dancing. She showed me herself in a white dress dancing and laughing. She said no matter how much she tried to fix her own pain in the long run it got the best of her. She ended up taking her own life and that of her unborn child as well, for she was pregnant from a colleague. This decision weighs heavily on her. Even in the afterlife.

There were a few others that tried to come through, but not as strong as those two. It got to the point where I was overwhelmed and had to tap out and stop. To try and paint you a picture of what I was seeing, imagine sitting at a busy park, like Central Park in New York, and hundreds of people are standing around you.

They are trying to come talk to you one by one but then they start overlapping each other and you are so crowded you feel like you are suffocating. That was the point it was getting to. I killed the music and packed up my notebook and headphones. I checked to see if SpiritTalker was getting anything. I had NO IDEA what SpiritTalker was getting and the fact a lot of what it got correlated with what I was seeing blew my mind. Talking about a boy, toys, dinosaurs, and stuff that went along the line of both when the child came through and when the nurse was talking to me. This blew my mind then and still blows my mind to this day. That connection is deep, and I am truly grateful for that experience.

Now, I am sad to say this chapter is about to come to an end. For I am to about to tell you about the last trip me and a friend took to this location. Well, at least the final Urbex (Urban Exploring) trip to Seaside. With the end of the road coming for these buildings, we wanted one last swing at going inside. Mostly because he wanted to see the inside of Maher at least once because he had not been in that one yet. When we arrived and saw they finally patched up the access to the admin building. I was so upset; I was ready to call it quits then and there. This one was my personal favorite of the two because it was the one I always had some kind of connection with spirits while inside. Which left only Maher, and even though I found this one a bit boring something inside me said "go for it." Which led to a trip I will never forget.

We got into the building and made our way to the basement. I wanted to get the sightseeing over with and get right to the communication part, because this is why I take these risks, to talk to the spirits, not the views. As much as I'm not in it for the sightseeing I will admit, these really old buildings are a perk. It builds to the atmosphere of exploring the unknown, the "creepy" vibes if you will. I have been in that basement a few times already and never found it to be on the spookier side, even when I was alone. Nothing could've prepared me for what was about to happen to us. Not only did this building get the best of my nerves that day but his as well.

We got the sightseeing of the basement done and were making our way out to head back up to the second floor and that's when the super eerie stuff began. We were about halfway out and almost at the stairs, when it sounded like the heat to the building was turning on. The pipes started hissing with steam. We were frozen in our tracks, listening, trying to comprehend what was going on. As we stood still I could hear laughter of children coming from behind my buddy, from where we had just come from. Every hair on my body was standing up; the goosebumps were head to toe. He asked me what the plan was, I told him to "get the hell out of the basement." We didn't hesitate anymore and made our way to the stairs. I wish I had the laughter on video, but he was talking in low tones so you can't hear it. However, there were two times I heard something I can't explain. Sounds like a reptile, while another was like a growl. I am kind of glad we didn't hear that in person.

We got back up to the second floor, and it was time to get down to business. We began setting up some equipment and getting ready for one last investigation inside Maher. I defaulted to SpiritTalker (you'll hear about this one the most) and ran it for a bit. We made our way to the side closer to the main entrance and switched to a Spirit Box (modified radio) to try and chat. As we were doing this, we could hear talking all around us and it was not through the radio. It sounded clear but distant at the same time. It was raining outside and there was no one walking around, just us. So, they were being chatty but not through the radio. The point that was on the wilder side was the singing we heard. I was talking, asking a question and as I did it sounded like a female was singing behind me. I quickly shut the Spirit Box off and we just sat in silence listening.

It sounded like chatter all around us as we sat in the silence listening to everything that was going on. While we were quiet, we captured an EVP on video saying, "just having some fun." These spirits were really messing with us. And they made it well known. After the quick excitement of the singing ghost, we thought about trying another floor, so we headed over to the stairs to go up to the third floor. To enter the third floor, you have to go through a big wooden door. As I slowly cracked it open, we both instantly got a “do not do it” vibe. As if something was telling us not to enter and go on that floor. I am not usually one to listen and will push the limits but when two of us both simultaneously got the same feeling, we sure as hell listened and let that wooden door close and headed back to the second floor.

This time we tried talking to them by the side where we had entered from. I went back to using communication tools and he had set up his REM-pod. REM-pods emit their own little electromagnetic field and react when something interrupts that “bubble.” The REM-pod triggered a few times, I always love seeing a REM-pod go off, and it’s probably one of my favorite nonverbal devices. We were also starting to get some good talking, but something deep down really kept saying it was time to go, and we were pushing our luck. After all that had happened in that short time span, I was not about to ignore the call to leave, so I thanked the ones who came and talked, we packed up and made our exit.

After our departure from Maher, we made our way to the wooden bridge to try and talk to them some more. The bridge that is placed in between both buildings. The bridge can be hit or miss. I’ve noticed it can be a way to catch spirits passing through to go to each building. We didn’t end up having that much luck this time. And with it raining on and off and having a constant sprinkle shower I didn’t want to get any gear ruined by walking around the grounds, so I called it a day. Not how wanted or expected the last exploration of this location to go but at the same time I wouldn't change a single thing about it.

# Chapter 2:

## AN UNWANTED GUEST

For the most part, and to the best of my ability, I am going to try to keep these chapters going forward in order of my exploring timeline, the order I did them in. Seaside, having a special sweet spot in my paranormal heart though, deserved that opening. Let's go to the start now, the beginning of it all with Urbex and paranormal. We are visiting the location that was my first, the cherry popper, the one that brought me to hell and back, Mansfield Training Facility and Hospital. I am not one to try and forget places and what I experienced at them, but if I could shake this one from the memory books, I would.

Opening its doors in 1860 it was originally known as Connecticut School for Imbeciles at Lakeville. In 1915 the name was changed to the Connecticut Training School for the Feeble Minded at Lakeville. Two years later it was merged with the Connecticut Colony of Epileptics which was founded in 1910 at Mansfield, which lead to its current name. It reopened its doors in 1917 as the merged facility.

When it reopened in 1917 there were a total of 402 students in residence. By 1932, the total number of residents had grown to 1,070. During The Great Depression and WWII, the demand for their services was so high that it resulted in overcrowding and a wait list to get in. In 1918/19 the institution was hit hard by the Spanish Influenza in which 200 out of 300 patients were infected by it. Resulting in 30 of them passing away. Only one doctor (Dr. LaMoure) and one nurse were put in charge of overseeing the infected.

The facility hit a high in the 1960's when there was a total of 1,609 patients/residents and 875 full-time staff members. During the 1970s and 80s many patients were relocated to other facilities and group homes dropping the resident count down to 1,106. By 1991 the total resident count was down to 141. In 1993 the facility closed its doors due numerous lawsuits placed against the facility for its conditions. Many of the buildings were demolished and the rest of the buildings were sectioned off for the University of Connecticut (UCONN) and the Bergin Correctional Institution that is right across the street from the old facility.

One of the lawsuits that was held against the facility was that of a former patient and she won. Glady Burr filed a lawsuit against the institution in 1979 for $125 million for the cruelty she faced while being there. There was denial of civil rights, and she claimed to be used for slavery. The worst part is, she was mentally stable. She was in there because her mother did not want her and had her tests of her mental state manipulated. She was awarded $235 thousand.

The lawsuit that got the facility shut down was the Conn. CARV v Throne case. It started in 1978 due to the allegations of cruelty of patients in the facility. The facility was practicing lobotomies and using straitjackets which we all know now is a cruel practice. This case was heavily investigated into the 90's and many patients were found with wrongfully placed DNR (Do Not Resuscitate) tags on them which led to the downfall of this location. The patients who were still there during the closing were relocated to community-oriented homes.

With that slight history lesson out of the way and now that you have a small idea of how "lovely" this place was while it was operational, let's dive into why this is one location I wish I could forget. It was the one to pop the Urbex cherry but doesn't mean I want

to go to prom with it. In fact, I would lock this one up in the Pandora's box of my memory bank and move

on if I could. By now, I have a taste for the paranormal experiences of my own by visiting the grounds of Seaside now I am at the point where I really want to go all out, get into these places and really explore what they have to offer.

I am all over social media looking for groups, posts of places that are more on the easier side of getting in, because let's face it. I want in and out. I want little to no concentration of sneaking around and more concentration of making connection with the spirits of the places. Bingo! I come across a post about this location, and a person was nice enough to share a pinpoint of where you can park to walk around. You can be on the grounds and look around but like every other abandoned, fenced off old building, going inside is a big no-no. He said it was fairly easy, and it was not too far from my home, so I packed up my camera, some gear, and headed on over.

Now, this is my first time, and I am about to go from not even tipping my toes in the pool to just straight up running and jumping in full cannonball. So, I am nervous beyond words. I can see all these amazing looking buildings with holes in the fences just there for the taking but I am hesitant to go through with it. I walk around the grounds, take some outside pictures and as I am doing so, something inside me said, "saddle-up. It's go time" so I made my way through the fence. I remember as I walked to the door of the first building seeing the bodies of dead animals decaying and thinking to myself, "this is a great sign."

I open the door and run inside. At this point I have so many thoughts racing through my mind. Like, turn on the flashlight (because it was boarded up well and dark in the first room), I hope there's no homeless people about to try and fight me for entering their home, but most of all, I hope scary ass spirits don't try to mess me up and hopefully it's Casper I get to meet. The adrenaline is coursing through my veins in overload and at the same time I am as excited as a child being let loose in a candy store. It is a rush that is hard to put into words.

I turned my flashlight on and made my way through the halls like Shaggy and Scooby. I was on full alert mode and ready to run if I needed to. Once the nerves settled a bit, I was able to concentrate on the energy of the place, the energy of spirit. Other than a few old building type noises, wind blowing through the empty halls, doors creaking from the wind there was not much going on. I got a few EMF spikes on the K2 meter but nothing crazy. At this point I had not learned about SpiritTalker (not sure if it was even out yet) so I went with the Spirit Box and voice recordings. The lack of energy levels I was picking up was being shown in the results of quiet recordings. So, I did a couple laps around each floor, took some pictures and left.

Across the way of the building, I had just explored is one of the hospital buildings. That bad Larry was next. I made my way over, went through the hole that was already provided by those before me and crawled through the open window. As soon as I entered that building you could feel the energy and I did not like the way it was feeling. Felt repressed, as even the spirits didn't want to talk about or remember the place. Angry, so much pain. And to my left and to my right was so much darkness. I felt like I was about to be run up on by a swarm and cornered like an injured animal, ripe for the taking. So, I said "nope" and went right back out that window, I knew not to do this one alone.

That was it for trip one. I got what I needed. A reason to go back, but play it smart, do it safe and have at least one other person with me.

So, I headed home to plan out a trip. As I was thinking of how to approach this beast, I was watching paranormal shows on television. I can't stand the over reactions and falsified information they give out a lot of the time, but they give me ideas of places to visit, almost like a vacation wish list. Well, I was watching one of those MOST HAUNTED LOCATIONS IN AMERICA type shows and it was of a lady who bought the house of who originally was one of the superintendents of Mansfield. As I'm watching this episode and seeing how messed up this episode was (they found bones in the basement, a medium picked up on rape, slavery, and murder) it clicked in my head, holy shit, that is the same Mansfield I was just at earlier the same day and now I know I shouldn't be going alone. There is most definitely some bad juju there.

So, like any logical person I find someone crazy enough to explore this place with me for trip two. It happened to be a cousin who was wanting to dabble in the paranormal and get out there for himself as well. I told him the level of messed up it was, the dark history of the place. I wasn't going to not tell him. It would be kind of messed up. Anyways, we coordinated a day to go, and we went to investigate the dorm building I had quickly checked out and the hospital.

This trip wasn't anything from an average trip. A few EVPs, some talk through the radio but as I said, a pretty average trip. I will say this though. It was the first one as a team in an abandoned location and we got to see how to maneuver in and out under the radar but get what we went there for. It added to our knowledge set and gave us enough to want to continue working with the location, which ended up leading to a few unforgettable trips. One of them together and two of them pushing the boundaries by going alone. As well as a trip with another friend.

The first I want to take you on was a solo trip. I am now at the point where I am more comfortable with going to places alone. I still know it is not the smartest thing to be doing, especially with the homeless or the fact that when you're alone you're more likely to get an attachment but I want to push myself to new boundaries. That and at this point I was discovering that relying on others to go with me was more of a project than what it is worth (there was some stuff going on behind the scenes with current partners) and I just want to explore and have some fun. So, I grabbed my gear and made my way to this old hospital to go one on one with my fears.

I arrive at my destination on a warm fall day. However, I don't go right to the housing building I have been through a few times already, instead I choose a new one. This one felt different. Felt more alive. I make my way through it, a perimeter check if you will. I want to make sure it is safe enough to stage up and try to talk to the spirits. I don't need any random surprises, well at least from the living. I checked all the floors and rooms, take a few pictures.

Not a person in sight. Just myself, alone in this building with an odd energy to it.

I am completely alone and getting ready to start when it sounded like someone slammed a door. I quickly grab my phone and go to my old Facebook page THE HAUNTED LAIR and start a live video. As soon as the LIVE video is up and running I tell people what had just happened and crack the joke, "if I'm going to die I want you to see what happened." I was trying to calm down from the jump-scare. During the live it gets more interesting. I was asking a question or saying something and an individual watching the live said she heard someone, not me, say something. A LIVE EVP!

However, I am not there for LIVE streaming and taking my attention away from the spirits, so I thanked those who jumped on to watch and get back to work. I am now running a Spirit Box and getting some that are willing to talk. Again, I hear some banging and now it sounds like someone is walking around. I quickly pack up in case someone is now in the building with me. I walk around while using SpiritTalker to continue to try to get someone to talk to me as I cautiously walk around to see if I can find who was making all the noise. NO ONE! There is no one around. I used the only good staircase to go up and down to each floor, I checked each room, even ran through the creepy dark basement floor checking each room, each hiding spot and still, I am alone.

I was feeling as if there was someone or something there who didn't want me there and was trying to scare me out. I will admit even though I was scared I was more against not wanting to push my luck. I listened to the warning and made my way out.

I wasn't ready to go home yet either. I put on my big boy pants, took a few deep breaths, paced back and forth for a good minute and then headed to face the hospital one on one.

I crawled through the windows that was opened for access. It was almost like déjà vu of the first time I walked into that building alone. Only this time I was not going to be scared off easily. I turned to the right and turned my flashlight on because the access hall was so dark I couldn't even see in front of my face. I made my way through the slight flooding of the ramped floor by walking over decayed pieces of the building and got to the hallway where there was light again. I shut my light off and thought I was in the clear. I was wrong, dead wrong. I could feel like there were so many people watching me curious as to why I was there and what I was doing.

I made my way down the hall and through the double doors that were there. Once you get through the double doors there is (or at least there was back then, I haven't been in four years) an old, broken, creepy-looking piano. I would go, set up a REM-pod by the double doors, and cat balls by another door that leads to a stairway up to the 2nd floor, or down to the basement and would use a Spirit Box to talk or record EVPs while messing with the broken piano. I can't play piano to save my life, but musical vibrations are almost magical when it comes to communicating with the other side.

As I was looking at the REM-pod by the double doors, I was also looking through the broken windows of the doors. And I swear on everything I saw a dark shadow coming right towards those doors walking the halls on the other side of me. I did not want to meet whoever or whatever that was, but it was blocking my exit. My only other option was to grab my gear and go up a floor. I was not about to head down to the blacked-out basement after what I just saw. I did just that. I grabbed my gear and got up to the second floor. This floor felt lighter, not alone but not as creepy. I let my nerves calm down and get back to trying to communicate with hopefully some more, less angry spirits.

Waiting to feel out the energy that I was trying to avoid I was doing what I call "walk and talk." That is where I walk around with the Spirit Box trying to find chatty souls versus sitting in one spot waiting for them to come to me. I started off in a room that was staged like a classroom. It had desks all lined up facing a "teachers" desk that had an old computer on it and a chalkboard behind the desk. Then I walked around the hallway and made my way to what looks like a living room/waiting room. Had a couch, what would've been nice rugs at the time and looked like patients would've sat in there waiting to be seen.

I was getting some chatter, but I was not about to sit in one place waiting to see if that shadow was trying to find me. Once I thought I had a clearing I went back to the first floor. Looking around a bit I felt out the energy, and I didn't feel what I had felt when I saw the shadow, it felt calmer now. So I walked at a quick pace, making a beeline for the exit. As much as I wish this was the worst story I have to share from this place, it is not. But it was definitely an unforgettable trip.

Let's move along to another crazy adventure. During this one my camera captured something I did not see until reviewing the footage. This was a trip I had made with my cousin. We went at nighttime on a full moon. Yes, I truly believe a few days up to and a few days after a full moon helps increase spiritual energy. If they can affect the rest of everything that goes on around us, why can't they help charge up the afterlife? Especially if it's just us in our energy forms which are no longer restricted to the laws of physics.

Anyways, with this trip we solely concentrated on the hospital building. We went right to the second floor. We tried to do a live session, however even though we had excellent reception the audio was distorted. Sounded like a broken radio, as if something was trying to stop us from doing what we were doing. And the reason I know it wasn't because we were live on Facebook, it was because even on normal video recordings several times the audio had been distorted in that building. I'm telling you; this place was no joke.

We were getting really high EMF readings on the meters, REM-pods going off, talking to us a lot via Spirit Box and SpiritTalker. Just as it was getting really good, we had to call it quits due to some circumstances on his end. It was personal and it's not my place to talk about. But I was so pissed off that we had to leave right there and then during one of our best visits to this location. The energy in that place was through the roof that night.

Even though the trip was short, I wasn't going to let this wild trip go to waste. I still tried to salvage what little footage we had for a YouTube video and that's when I saw something I have never seen before, and still have not seen again, even to this day. We had a video camera with night vision staged in the hallway facing down towards the way out. As we were in a room doing the live session you see this self-illuminating light slowly coming up off of the floor, and it sits there for a quick moment of time before just vanishing into nowhere. I can't even try to put into words what that was and logically explain it. Forever an eerie mystery.

Which brings us to the trip that brought me to hell and back. If you have been following me along this journey via my socials you know where I am

about to go with this one. This is the trip where I got an attachment. A spirit that followed me home and gave me six lovely months of "fun." I am almost afraid to go into depth about this trip because I don't want to chance him coming back. But here goes nothing.

January 5th, 2021, I am at work and I get the news that my uncle, my godfather had passed away four days before my birthday. I am a wreck. It was also the year I had to renew my license, which I waited until that Saturday (my birthday) to go do, and Mansfield Training Facility was about twenty minutes away from the DMV. As much of a wreck as I was, I didn't want to be bummed out and made the mistake of going to the hospital. The mistake wasn't going itself but going while being in a moment of distress. When you are angry or sad you lower your vibrations, your wall of protection, essentially this makes you more susceptible to attachments.

Of course, I'm not thinking straight and go anyways. I have gone and seen mediums who have told me (and I know this myself from evidence) that loved ones on the other side go with me to places. They have fun with it like I do. I even remember as I entered the hospital I was saying, "This one is for you Uncle, now you can see what I do for fun." And in I went.

I didn't make it a long trip because it was only about twenty degrees outside and I wanted to go home and spend my birthday with family. My mother-in-law was also bringing over a lasagna for me. She makes me one every year for my birthday; she is the best! This was more of a quick trip to cheer me up and have some fun. I knew this was going to be quick, so

I headed right to that busted old piano and set up a REM-pod by the double doors. I was playing, well just hitting some keys and said, "come on, let's have some fun" and as I did the REM-pod by the doors started freaking out. It had never gone off here, especially to my awful piano playing skills so it caught me off guard and made me jump quick.

I said, "No fucking way. Thank you," for them setting it off. My birthday was starting to look up. I tried the piano a little longer and with no such luck I went upstairs for a quick visit. I went to the waiting room and threw some cat balls on the couch and was using SpiritTalker. The cat balls went off a few times and then I started getting warnings of "be careful" "evil" and more along the lines of bad spirits around and I shouldn't be there. At that point my nose was running bad, and I was having major sniffles from the cold and my fingertips were going numb. With the numbing of the cold and warnings of bad spirits around I took the opportunity to call it; trip over.

On the way home my leg felt as if something was crawling all over it. I felt dead to the world, what we call a paranormal hangover. It was so bad with the leg I had to pull over to make sure there was not an infestation of bugs crawling over me. I didn't think there were any since it was the dead of winter and there usually aren't any, but I didn't want to risk it. I pulled over and checked, nothing. No rashes, no bugs, no irritated bumps, nothing. Even as I'm looking, I can feel something crawling on my leg, but nothing is there. I get back in my car, and my radio starts acting up. I said "fuck off, you're not allowed to follow me," because now my human EMF is going off and I know I am not alone. Radio goes back to normal and the crawling feeling on my legs starts to go away, so I think I'm in the clear.

Something in the back of my mind though was telling me otherwise, but I didn't listen and shrugged it off. I got home, put on warm clothes, put the REM-pod and piano moment on TikTok (because I thought it was cool. The video quickly shot up to 700k views; a lot for me only having like 100 followers before posting it) and went to celebrate my birthday with the family.

Later I started to notice that whenever I get home, especially when I am at my computer working on videos I go from wide awake to instantly tired and miserable. I start thinking it is from work, not that there is a grumpy ass old man spirit draining me every time I am home. We are now getting closer to spring again, and at this point the draining is getting so bad it is starting to feed me with suicidal thoughts; I have suffered from depression a lot growing up, another sign I am overlooking. Nonetheless, I go to Mansfield again with another friend.

A cool trip; had a few EVPs, Spirit Box chatter, REM-pods going off, but the part of this trip that stands out is the little crank style music box I found and took home. I know this is a no-no, but I have a small collection from haunted places at home and wanted to add to it. Well, I get home and place it next to another music piece I have and go to the kitchen to make a sandwich. Out of nowhere I hear something smash. I instantly go to blame the kids for jumping around but they are sitting down, watching TV so now I'm confused about what just happened.

I head to what was my "man cave" at the time, where the box was and one of the pictures, I had of my kids was tossed halfway across the room onto the floor. I am thinking to myself, great I brought home a haunted item. I bring the music box back outside, throw it in my car and clean up the glass. The next day after work I bring it back, but now, I am honestly scared for the first time and refuse to go alone and a coworker I knew has been wanting to see these places, so I told him to go in with me. We get to the hospital, and I put the music box back exactly where I had found it and give him a quick tour of the basement all the way up to the second floor before we leave.

It is now almost six months now after my uncle's passing, the trip to Mansfield I shouldn't have taken and the depression and suicidal thoughts are getting to the point where they are almost stronger than myself. So, I go out to more places and explore the paranormal because they are always quick boosts of adrenaline that I need to distract myself. At home though, the feelings and thoughts start to come on a lot quicker, a lot stronger, almost like a virus is overtaking me. Now that I am a little more healed from my uncle's departure from the physical world and my intuitive side is getting back to normal, I begin noticing that when I am home, I feel something is lurking in the shadows, but I keep telling myself, it's all in my head. I tried to ignore it. My wife even tried telling me that she was picking up on something, someone hiding in my room. I told her she was crazy; I didn't want to acknowledge it.

That all changed during a full moon. I was trying to develop the intuitive side, make it stronger, and I was going to classes on how to get better with our natural gifts. Investigating with technology is cool and all, but I want those deeper, stronger connections with spirits while I am at locations. So I start meditating more, inner self-healing more and would do so even more with full moons. I will never forget this one meditation. As I was focusing on clearing my mind, I was envisioning a white space, a space cleansed of all the daily bullshit. And as I got my mind clear, and I was seeing all white and feeling the warmth of meditating, he showed me his face. The spirit that was attached to me made himself well known.

It wasn't a slow form showing up, it was jump-scare fast, like BOO, I'm here! I opened my eyes and was like, "what the fuck was that? Go away." I closed my eyes again and get myself back to my calm state and he does it again. This time as he does it my back starts to instantly burn, like someone just put a cigarette out on me, but it was my whole back that burned. I open my eyes back up, blow out my candles, shut my Himalayan salt rock lamp off, and head to the bathroom to take a shower. I take my shirt off and look at my back and there are scratch marks going across my whole back.

I am now scared out of my mind. I'm done ignoring it but at the same time I don't want to acknowledge him to give him more power. Like I am acknowledging his presence without showing fear. So, I keep my cool and get in touch with my friend who has been teaching me, an amazing medium, for help. She comes over to help us cleanse our place. She made me concentrate and focus on the spirit to find out where he came from and what he wants. She already knew the answer but was using it as a learning experience. This was when I was really working on my mediumship, and she was one of my teachers. At first my mind was racing as I had been to so many locations over the last few months. But once I cleared my mind, it all came forward.

He was from Mansfield and wanted my energy, my life force. What spirits will do sometimes is show you messages by showing something you can connect with, and being a comic book fan, he did just that. He showed me being overtaken by Venom which is an alien symbiote from Spider-Man. He finds a host he can bond with while slowly taking the life of the host, almost like a disease. And I told her what I was seeing, and she said that's exactly what was going on. That is what he wanted. I was there during a time when my spiritual shield was weak, and it was easy for him to attach to me like a leech. All he wanted was energy, my energy and always stayed in my room, waiting for me. Now that we know where he is from and why he is there, she helps cleanse more and helps him move along to a location nearby because it has way more energy for him to feed off. And it worked. Within a few days I was feeling more like myself, back to normal.

I have yet to go back to Mansfield since that moment and I refuse to go back. I know now that I am stronger and more prepared for a place like that, but it is not a chance I am willing to take. Lesson learned, never go to a haunted place when you're upset, even if you have the right intentions for that visit. Only go when your mind is cleared, focused, and you can keep your positive vibes high. I am still sad that I lost out on that music box from there for no reason though lol.

# Chapter 3:

## WELL HELLO BOB

Now that I we've gone through one amazing location and that hellish one, I want to visit the first ever abandoned exploring I did while trying to capture some paranormal evidence. It was the summer of 2021, and I wanted to really expand where I was going and the places I am seeing. I had caught wind of an abandoned Cold War base in the Cape Cod and wanted to check it out. The grounds are legal, because it is a state park and you can walk around and view it from outside the fence. This base never got to see war time action, but I know somehow, someway everywhere is haunted. People have been walking these grounds for hundreds of years before us in this current moment of time, it's just a matter of connecting with them. Being new to this at the time I didn't have much gear; a K2 meter, Spirit Box, and Voice recorders. I wasn't expecting any kind of contact, but I was hopeful.

In the windswept coastal sands of Cape Cod, Massachusetts, nestled within the town of Truro, lies a story of hidden history and the echoes of a bygone era. The North Truro Air Force Base was established during World War II, a period when the world was engulfed in conflict and the skies were seen as vital battlegrounds. Originally built in 1945 as a training facility for the United States Army Air Forces, this base played a crucial role in preparing pilots for the rigors of combat. The expansive grounds and runways of the base welcomed young men who yearned to serve their country, all while soaking in the salty breeze that whipped through the tall grasses of the surrounding landscape.

As the war drew to a close in 1945, the base began to evolve. It transitioned from a training facility into an essential part of the Cold War strategy. In 1951, the Air Force took over the operations, and North Truro became a critical site for radar operations, part of the larger DEW (Distant Early Warning) Line that monitored the skies for any potential threats. The radar installations that sprouted atop the hills stood like vigilant sentinels, ensuring that the Eastern Seaboard was protected from the specter of enemy aircraft. Local residents spoke in hushed tones about the beeping signals and flashing lights that peppered the night sky, marking a time when the world felt both perilous and strangely alive with drama.

Yet, the heart of North Truro Air Force Base was not solely encapsulated in military missions. The base fostered a unique sense of community as families settled into the area, forming a vibrant tapestry of life amid the armed forces. Social events, local fairs, and educational initiatives flourished on and off the base, bringing a sense of normalcy and camaraderie to those who lived in this isolated yet spirited environment. School

children mingled with military brats, and friendships blossomed, creating bonds that would stretch far beyond the transient nature of military life.

The 1960s brought significant changes to the operations of the base. With technological advancements rendering some installations obsolete, the Air Force began to downsize. By 1994 with the end of the Cold War, the North Truro Air Force Base was officially closed, leaving behind a vast expanse of land, scattered buildings, and the profound memories etched into the hearts of those who once called it home. It was a bittersweet farewell to a place that had encapsulated both the challenges of war and the warmth of community, as families packed their belongings and said their goodbyes.

In the years that followed, the site found new life. Portions of the old base were repurposed, becoming public spaces that welcomed beachgoers, birdwatchers, and history enthusiasts alike. Trails wove their way through the historic grounds, and the preserved radar towers whispered stories of days long past while standing as reminders of the site's pivotal role in national defense. Local historians recognized the need to document the rich tapestry of life around the base, ensuring that the sacrifices and struggles of those who served were not forgotten.

Today, visitors to North Truro can immerse themselves in the history that unfurls along its coastal paths. Signs detail the base's expansive narrative, highlighting both its military significance and its lasting impact on the community. The area has transformed from a military stronghold into a sanctuary of nature and history, inviting new generations to explore the legacy of those who once soared through the skies and the families who built a life amidst the uncertainty of wartime. Through its transition, North Truro has become a reminder that even the most formidable structures can fade, but the stories they carry endure, interwoven within the very fabric of the land they once occupied.

I mentioned that some chapters may be on the shorter side due to the number of times I have visited them and the number of paranormal experiences I had in my time of visiting them. This is one of those chapters. I have only been to this location one time and that was back in 2021. I have wanted to go back because of how well the first trip went but I have heard through the grapevine that they watch this location a lot better now. So, unfortunately this was a one and done location. Still an unforgettable experience nonetheless, I just wish I had more to share from here for you all. I never put out videos of this location, just some pictures I took, and I do not want to let this one go to waste and just sit forever untold on my computer.

It was myself, my cousin, and his girlfriend. We took a nice road trip to go explore this once blooming air force base to see what it had to offer. It is almost towards the tip of Cape Cod. For me it is about two and a half hours each way. So, like I said, I had high hopes this trip was going to be worth it and it was. It was a lovely spring day, nice and warm, sun blazing strong. A day that was made for exploring. We arrived at our destination and parked down in the designated parking area and made our way up towards base. There are baseball fields there and a path dedicated for walking around what remains of the base. There were people hiking the trail, some walking their dogs and with it being close to the ocean, the air felt amazing.

It being our first time being there and about to do some Urbex we walked the site up and down trying to see if it was doable. Plus, the place was massive, and we wanted to see all that it had to offer. I was starting to feel hopeless because we couldn't find any openings; a way to enter. As we got towards the end of the massive loop that wraps around the base we saw people running around drunk and asked them how they got in and they told us exactly where to go. We followed their directions and there it was! An opening! The opening was not fun though, especially being a well-rounded guy. It was a hole that was dug into the ground under the fence, almost like what a dog will do. Somehow I managed to get my heavy-set body through though and it was a walk in the park from there.

The entrance we used was on the housing side. A mini community if you will. The housing they would use for higher ranking officers and their families. Growing up I loved the Jurassic Park movies and to me being there reminded me of the second movie, The Lost World. All the houses were taken back by nature, and I was in complete awe seeing it all. Each house was wide open. You can tell they were boarded up at one point but can see many before us made them all accessible. It was also sad to see all the destruction brought on by the careless, and all the graffiti. People are disgusting when they destroy history like that.

We walked through the first house we came across, it felt so still, so quiet therefore I didn't try anything in that one. Same with house number two. It was about three or four houses in that the energy started feeling different. By house number three I had the Spirit Box out with a portable speaker that it came with and my K2 Meter. Nothing was coming through though. That all changed with house number four. From the moment we walked through that one and the rest of the trip I felt as if we were being followed, being watched carefully. I even tried going live on Twitter (now X) but the reception was so bad it did not work well at all. We were getting talk through the Spirit Box and K2 Meter was starting to pick up readings so I thought it would be cool to show it via live streaming.

I tried some voice recordings but didn't notice anything on the playbacks. However, when reviewing the footage on my cousin's camera there was indirect EVPS. Which validates that it is haunted. But why?

Who? Are they members of the forces that were so dedicated to the military that they still take up post, even in the afterlife? These questions started racing through my mind as I reviewed the footage and still to this day. It was starting to get late in the afternoon and there was so much to still explore that we visited another house or two before heading to the next area. Still, feeling that being followed feeling I remember constantly looking behind me, looking for who was following us.

On our way out we found a hole in the fence which I was beyond relieved about especially because this big guy did not feel like having more fence dig into my rolls. We made our way to the other part of the base where the community buildings and shared housing buildings were. Again, we ran into the issue of finding a way to slip in and out. We found what looked like an attempt at digging under the fence, but I was NOT squeezing this big old body in that itty bitty hole in the ground, so somehow it may have been enlarged enough for us to get in. The first building that was opened for us to explore was an old bowling alley. That was a quick in and out.

From there we headed over to a building that looked like it would've been used for shared living. This one was a bit more boarded up so it was a little darker in there even with plenty of sunlight still shining down on us. Again, feelings of being followed, and the K2 meter was going off again. Who is following us? What do they want? I tried to use the Spirit Box again to find out who our mysterious follower was but got nowhere. Whoever was following us was trying to not let it be known, but the vibes were giving them away. We then made our way into what looked like a fancy chow hall. There was not much left to this one and Mother Nature had this one in very rough shape. So we didn't waste much time in here, but we made sure to take in the views.

By then, the sun was starting to set. I remember the views of watching the sun setting over this base that once thrived now left to rot away. It was breathtaking. That's where this trip takes a slight not so happy turn. We find a building that was sitting by itself almost dead center of the grounds. So, we wanted to check it out as well. I lead the way on this one and it was instant regret. As soon as I opened the door and got about 2ft in I got punched in the face by some kind of chemical. It was so overwhelming that it was instantly choking me. I almost plowed my cousin and his girlfriend over running back out of there, for they were still by the doorway. I had to gasp for air and drink some water and sit for a good minute to get over what I just went through.

With that building not being accessible and nothing else to explore we just walked up and down the grounds enjoying the sun set. Now with night upon us the base was starting to feel eerie. It felt as though the place pulled a 360 on us. Like Jekyll and Hyde. With the long ride home we still faced we thought it would be good to call it quits. As we made our departure, something was drawing me back into the bowling alley building and it was on the way out, so we went back in for one last swing. I could still feel that someone had been following us and I wanted to know who it was. At this point the alley is pitch black, so I was hoping to finally get some answers. If they wanted to remain hidden, the darkness was the perfect way to maybe finally get them to talk.

The K2 meter is going even higher in readings now, and I felt as if someone was getting closer to us, almost right on top of us. I had my cousin go on the Facebook page I had made at the time and livestream it for people to watch. I knew something was going to happen just not sure what. As the K2 meter started to go higher I said, "I know you are there, can we get a name please?" and we didn't hear anything at this time, but I thought I heard someone breathing by me, I am starting to get scared. There is no one in there just the three of us. But the people who were watching the live feed heard a man whisper "Bob" after I asked for a name.

My cousin finished the live feed and we made our departure. After we made it on the other side of the fence we were reviewing the livestream to see who was watching and trying to interact with it and that's when we saw people heard "Bob" when I asked for a name. I was like "What? No way!" So, we found the timestamp of the comment and there it was, crystal clear. A live EVP! I was blown away and will never forget that moment. I wish I had this on video to share but my cousin forgot to save a hard copy of the video to his phone before submitting it to Facebook and due to some personal reasons he had to delete the account he used to livestream on which in turn deleted the video. The only ones who witnessed this incredible moment were those watching it as it happened and the three of us before the video was forever deleted.

If I knew I could easily get in and out of this location I would go back in a heartbeat, no questions asked. Because who is Bob? Why was Bob following us? Why is he still there? Are there more spirits there as well? If so, who? I hate it when a location leaves more questions than it gives answers (which happens a lot) and I would love to learn more about them, their stories.

# Chapter 4:

## NO, YOU CAN NOT HAVE MY SOUL

The next location we are visiting has a book written by another investigator from her experience there. She got an attachment from something and it took her a good amount of time to get rid of it. It was an attachment that made her life a living hell. A good friend of mine who is a caretaker at a famous location in Massachusetts is friends with her as well and has a copy of the book. I told her about going there and she let me borrow the book so I could see just how fun this place can be and to be careful. I have only been to it a few times, but it's a place I refuse to go back to. The last trip I took I had something not so human following me, trying to attach to me, in fact I don't even like driving by this location anymore or close to it, because of that moment. Not only did I skim that book of this investigator's attachment, but I listened to her tell her experience about it on a paranormal related podcast and it opened my eyes to what I was dabbling in by going to this place. We are about to head on over to the second abandoned location I ever explored, The Rutland Prison Camps.

The Rutland Prison Camps, located in Rutland, Massachusetts, have a complex history rooted in the correctional system of the state. Established in 1896, these camps were originally intended as a means of housing prisoners in a sustainable environment while allowing them to engage in productive labor. It was a prison made for those of lesser convictions. Nestled in the woods of central Massachusetts, the remote location provided an opportunity for prisoners to work on forestry and agriculture projects, contributing to the local economy while also serving as a form of rehabilitation.

Over the years, the Rutland Prison Camps evolved in their approach to incarceration and rehabilitation. The camps operated under the premise that productive work could lead to better outcomes for inmates, reducing recidivism rates. From the start, the prison system focused on providing inmates with vocational training and skills that could potentially help them reintegrate into society upon their release. In addition to food production, inmates participated in a variety of woodworking and crafts, helping to build structures and provide other goods for local use. They even helped farm and produce milk for Worcester County along with some vegetables on their vegetation farm.

I know someone who also told me about a darker story from this location. I forgot who he knows or who he had connections within this prison camp, but he shared what he knew with me. If I remember correctly, I think it was someone he knows that worked for the town or a division that worked with the camps. I tried finding out more about what he shared with me online but had no luck. He told me the mafia would pay off guards to hide bodies in the prison grounds. With the history of the mafia, and how many people feared them and how many crooked cops there are out there it is easy to believe. What makes me believe these stories even more though, is the EVPs I have heard, and the communication we got over ITC while visiting that talk about secrets, murder, and rape. Even communication from the spirits here about hidden bodies.

Most of the camp is destroyed, laid to rest in the soil, given back to Mother Nature to reclaim. However, there are still some buildings and foundations you can see if you take a trip through the once thriving prison grounds. It has been closed and left to nature since 1930. If you take a trip to see it for yourself, keep in mind of hunting seasons for many people hunt in the woods nearby. I recommend going early spring or late fall, when most of the green is gone and tall grass is dead because all that is left of some buildings is the ground level foundations and nature hides them well once the

overgrowth is back.

I've made a few trips to this location before cutting it off. I even refuse to go back for pictures, and because I really don't go for the sightseeing most the pictures of this location will be screenshots of the documented footage. I have been in fall, spring, and summer and each time was an amazing view, but when I know what lies on the other side for me here, it makes the eagerness to go back slim to none. I can't even drive close to this location without weird stuff happening to me in my car as I pass by. The first two trips I had here were the best and those will be the ones I have you take a stroll down memory lane with me too.

Rutland Prison Camps is totally legal to visit from sunrise to sunset. I don't get the daylight restrictions on woods, but it is what it is. If I were to guess I would say it is so you do not get injured walking the grounds at night. People cannot even handle walking around the daytime without getting hurt, yes it has happened. I wanted a place to go to that would really push me and not have to worry about getting caught. I had read about this one online and thought it would be a good starter, a good one to really start developing as an investigator. An abandoned prison camp, where could I go wrong?

I am an early bird when it comes to these adventures, so, I grabbed my cousin early in the morning and made sure to get there as the sun was rising. It was really eerie as we slowly drove through the woods to the site down the dirt road in the fog. I could feel the energy of this place growing stronger as we got closer and I did not know what to expect. I found a good spot to park, and we headed on our way to explore the ruins.

We walked around for a bit. We did not try investigating right away because we wanted to see if there were any buildings left. I knew it didn't matter either way because the grounds are haunted, but I wanted to explore a bit. Remember how I said people even manage to get hurt in the day? I witnessed it first-hand. My cousin was walking and either taking pictures and videos on his phone or getting his camera set up as we were walking and stepped right into a hole in the foundation we were walking over. He totally wiped out, pretty dang well too. Luckily no injuries occurred but damn, I wouldn't have wanted to take the trip that he did.

We got the sightseeing done. We had walked around and looked around enough. Now was time to start talking to the ones we could feel walking all around us. Find out who was eager to talk to us. We made our way up the dirt road that led to what looked like an area that would have been used to store vegetables. It is an area that looks like it was a stable. It is cut into the hill, as if the coolness of the mountain and shade would've been a good place to store the vegetables.

The back wall, furthest from the entrance, has a nice sized hole in it. I put a voice recorder in it and staged a REM-pod on the ground. From there I went to set up with a Spirit Box. It was almost instant with the chatter that was coming through. You can tell there were some that were very eager to talk. It was so busy that it was overwhelming trying to keep up with them all. I was starting to think maybe the Spirit Box was broken so after a little I switched over to Necrophonic. Necrophonic is an ITC application that can be used for communication. It can be downloaded both on iOS and Android for a one-time purchase.

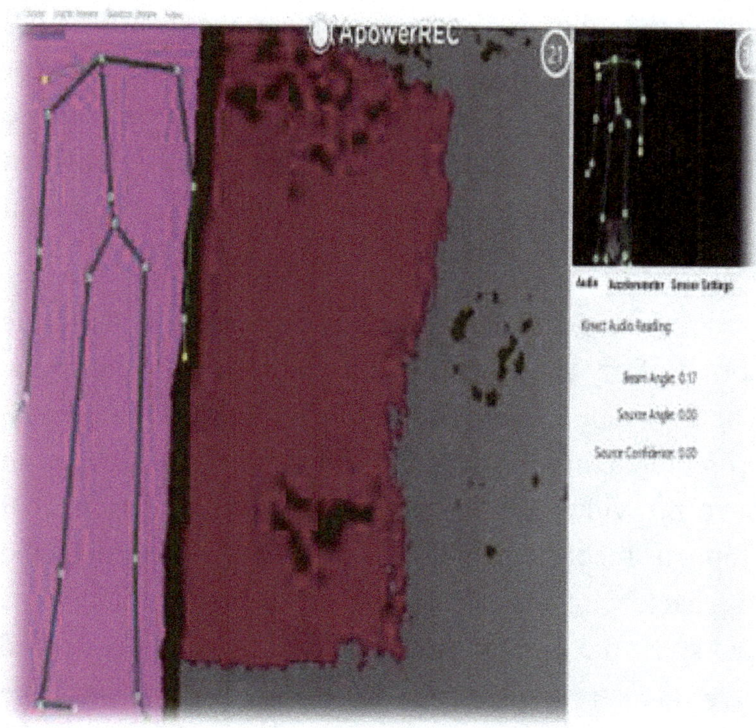

Same thing! They were so eager to talk and overlapping each other it was almost impossible to understand most of it. I will admit that when it comes to talking communication through ITC apps and Spirit Boxes I can miss some stuff but dang, this was impossible. It was so bad I was getting a little frustrated. I wanted to know what they were saying but they were making it extremely difficult.

We gave it the good 'ol college go but we were getting nowhere. So, I sat for a minute trying to feel out where we should try next to talk to them. See where I was drawn to. This feeling led us to the only semi still standing building. Looks like the remains to an old holding cell building. I really hope those cells were for the more severe or prisoners being punished because these cells are an inhumane size. And you can tell when that building was fully intact there was little to no light getting into those cells.

As we were setting up in one of the cells in the corner of my eye I saw a shadow figure run right by us. The first time I ever witnessed an apparition in person, no pictures, and no video but in person! I happened to have my video camera pointing in that direction, so I stopped recording and when I went to watch the playback with my cousin the file was corrupted! Was that spirit the one I was drawn to? The reason I wanted to go investigate at the cell block building? It was time to get our equipment going.

We had our K2 meters out; he had one and I had one. Both of them were picking up random spikes of energy. I put a voice recorder on the ground and while that was recording, we had video cameras going as well. I wanted to see if it would capture voices and maybe our Spirit Box sessions more clear for when we played them back while reviewing. I don't ever really do this, like at all, but it paid off.

We were having same issue as the last session. A lot of chatter and way too fast to keep up with. However, the voice recorder heard it all, so it was easier to understand while listening to the recording with headphones.

The Necrophonic got a lot of chatter, and it sounded like spirits having conversations amongst themselves. That is the first time I noticed that maybe if we just sit and listen, we can get their stories just being quiet and letting them talk. I know we like to ask direct questions and get direct responses, but silence can be bliss.

Also, as I was doing the playbacks, I noticed it picked up a couple of EVPs as well. Not the Necrophonic. And not my cousin and I talking. Between both the Necrophonic and the EVPs there was talk of murder. Talk of Rape. You can hear them talking about taking money for bad deals and deeds. There were also voices saying stuff about not harming us, to leave us alone. Talking about whether we should leave, that it is not safe for us. Were there spirits on the other side protecting us? If so, from who or what?

We had missed so much, we thought we were getting nowhere while we were at these ruins. I admit it, it does happen, you always seem to catch more after leaving than you thought but this was bad. How could we have missed that much? We ended this trip by trying to investigate in what looked like a tunnel that has slightly caved in or possibly an underground storage area. It is narrow and not that long and I was eager to see if anyone would chat with us one last time.

This session was a little easier to understand. Most of them were asking for help, saying they were stuck. This helped me for the second visit. If they were stuck and needed help, I was going to try my best to grant those wishes. What I found the most interesting of this session was the Mel Meter readings I was getting while we were in there. A Mel Meter reads electromagnetic fluctuations like a K2 tries to but is more reliable and gives a digital read out versus colored LED lights. It will read temperatures as well. Newer models can be purchased that include a REM-pod mode as well. This is one of my favorite tools to use. Three tools in one device.

While we were in the tunnels the base line reading "normal range" was reading around a .6. Low energy, nothing crazy. It is always good to walk around and see what the average range is.

What kept getting me excited, and I found interesting as we were getting answers through Necrophonic, the readings on the Mel Meter would go from .5, .6 to 20.5 or higher. There was one point it jumped over 50! This is high! And I loved that it was as it felt like people walking by me towards my cousin who was in front of me with the Necrophonic and getting our responses. There was one point it felt like someone was standing next to me and the whole time the Mel Meter stayed around 20-30 for a readout. It was not going up and down, it was staying consistent.

At this point I was starting to feel tired. We had been there for a couple of hours, and I was ready to call it quits. We thanked the spirits for talking to us and packed it up. As I reviewed the footage at home I noticed in the vegetable storage area the same thing, a lot of cries for help, being stuck. At this time I was just starting to take mediumship classes in person and reading as much as I could online about it, therefore I knew it was possible to help spirits move on and I wanted to try and give it a go. It is not on us, the physical to cast judgment on a spirit and what they did in their physical life. It is for those on the other side to cast judgment, the higher powers to be.

I was new to the field at this time so at first I was in almost every paranormal social I could find. Now, I can't stand them for how toxic they can be, like almost everyone in this field can be. So, I am in little to none now. It was nice to see what others were doing and learning from different experiences. Now, I just ignore it all and do my own thing. But this is how I found out about National Ghost Hunting Day. It is the last Saturday of September, the official kick off to the Spooky Season. With me finding this out last minute it was impossible to find a "pay to play" location that still had availability. And with us wanting to go back to Rutland for a follow-up trip, I thought it would be a good one for us to do.

This trip was going to be different. This trip I had a plan; we were not going in as a bunch of rookies but determined to help those who we can. I had just built my own SLS Camera and wanted to give it a good test run as well. We got back to the old camps but this time we visited the cemetery that is off in the woods for those who perished there first. I tell the spirits what the game plan is, to go to the old prison and try to let them share their stories and before we leave, I would try to help those who wanted to move on do so. That it wasn't a forced passing over but there for those who truly wanted the help.

After our brief visit to the cemetery, we headed to the ruins of the prison to begin the investigation and then try to help the ones who are stuck. Even with this day being back in 2021 almost 5 years ago now, I can still remember how gorgeous it was outside. Towards the end of September in New England it can be a hit or miss temperature-wise. It is either already cooling down to fall temps or really hot with left over summer heat. This day was perfect and the sun shining brightly made it even better.

We made our way right to the vegetable storage area again and started there. I got my SLS Camera up and running. As I was panning around to make sure it was good to go and making sure it was recording, I caught a figure that was moving, almost as if it was crawling along the walls. Every hair on my body started to stand up. I acknowledged whomever I was catching on my SLS and that's when it gets weird. My SLS froze on the stick figure as I was following it and then instantly died. The tablet was fully charged and the batteries powering the Kinect piece were brand new, yet it was dead. I thought it was fried; I couldn't even get it to turn on enough to show any indication of "low battery." I couldn't get it to show anything at all.

However, once we left the grounds it turned on no problem. So, was I catching something that wanted to remain hidden? Did it kill my SLS long enough to avoid being exposed? When reviewing the footage, I noticed something eerie that I cannot explain, clawing sounds. I was recording the stick figure and the wall with my phone, getting non SLS footage and as this figure is moving along the wall you hear clawing, as if something with long nails were scraping along the surface. Was this a non-human entity?

I was beyond upset about the SLS; I had busted my ass making it, just for it to shut down like that. I fought with the thing for a good five minutes or so before giving up. I even fought with it some more at the holding cells when we made our way to them after the storage area. With the SLS out of the picture we reverted back to some cat balls and Necrophonic.

I was trying to see who killed my SLS on me, it refused to come forward. I then turned my attention back to helping those who felt stuck and offered a crossing over to those who truly wanted it. I placed my phone on the ground while running Necrophonic and closed my eyes. I said if you really want out and want help crossing over form a single file line and come state your name, so I know who to include in the prayers when I try to help you cross over. I had my eyes closed and I could see silhouettes of individuals lining up in front of me. And almost instantly through Necrophonic names started coming through.

I know the spiritual side is capable of things that are absolutely mind blowing and this was my first real experience like that. Seeing the spirits of people coming forth via mediumship and having technology validate what I was seeing was hard to grasp at the time. It almost felt as if it was a dream. Once the crowd slowed down, I told them where we were going next and to follow along. We went back to the cell blocks to try and get more information based off of our last visit.

We were back to square one. Even with us asking more direct questions about the mafia and other stuff that was mentioned in trip one it was a free for all on their end. We would get bits and pieces of what we were trying to gather but nothing too coherent. More hints of being paid off, bad deeds, secrets, and once again more cries for help. I knew that it was going to be almost impossible to get full cooperation, so I offered the help again to those who wanted it and told them to follow us.

We made our way back to the broken tunnel/underground storage. To this day I still do not know what it is, but that's what it looks like. It had been raining a lot, so it had stored a good amount of water in there. That being so, I got in enough to tell whoever was in there the same thing. If they wanted help to follow us, that it was not a forced offering. I looked around for a bit, tried to feel out an area that would be good to do the prayer. And that's when I found some foundation that was not covered much by trees and the sun was shining brightly over the area.

We lit some incense to try and cleanse the area as much as possible and found a wall to sit on. I envisioned a white light to surround me and the area for protection while calling upon archangels and my spirit guides to help with the process. Once I knew the safety net was in place, and I was protected by those on the other side I began calling out to those who wanted to cross over. I told them not to be afraid that they would be protected during their passage.

I had found a protection prayer online, a prayer for safe passage and was reciting it over and over. I was in complete awe as to what I was witnessing, it was almost distracting. I kept my focus and kept at it. I have bad anxiety which acts like severe ADHD, so this was a big moment for me to be able to stay this focused. I can still remember this like it just happened.

I could see an archangel casting a ring of fire around us, casting a safe passage. Another archangel helping spirits come over to the light with my dad and other spirit guides. I was watching the silhouettes of the spirits come within the ring of fire and slowly hover up towards a tunnel of light. To try and let you understand what I was seeing, you ever see a movie or a television show and someone is looking into a light so bright they can barely see and someone is walking towards them but the light makes it hard to see the individual. All they can really see is the outline of the person that looks like a shadow walking towards them? That's what it looked like. And I was watching them walk right towards a tunnel brighter than the sun and vanishing.

I can't tell you exactly how many I watched come towards the light, but it was a good amount. It felt like I was only doing this for like two minutes but in all actuality it was closer to thirty minutes before I had to stop. I was feeling drained. It was the first time I ever attempted this, and it took a toll on me. Towards the end though I remember watching this dark figure that could cross the fire circle and was pacing around it, angrily. It was not happy that I was helping spirits cross over, but I didn't care. I went until I physically and mentally couldn't anymore. You could feel a calming atmosphere all around us when I stopped.

As soon as I finished I made sure to use sage and cleanse myself a lot. I had no idea what it was trying to stop me, and I did not want to risk an attachment. I feel as it was the entity that killed my SLS camera, something trying to remain hidden. After the cross over mission, we called it a day. I was wiped and wanted to go home.

I have been back to Rutland a time or two after this and I still get activity because I know there are plenty of spirits who still remain on those grounds. I was excited to see a REM-pod work there since I tried the other times I went with my cousin and had no such luck with that or the chatter through the Spirit Box. But the two moments that stand out the most from those trips are etched in my mind. And one of them is the reason I will never go back. Well, I say that but as I write this I am tempted to go back one last time to see how different it is.

One of the moments was with a friend and her two kids. We had just gone to Mansfield and had a short-lived visit, so we went over to Rutland because we still had plenty of time for exploring. We walked around for a bit because they had never been and wanted to check it out. We walked around and finally made it to that half tunnel/underground storage and this is where it took a turn that I will never forget.

We were all about halfway in and out of nowhere I got a scent of sulfur, like eggs that had been rotting away for years. And it was a gorgeous day out, fresh air all around us and it was instantaneously gone and replaced by this wretched smell. With the snap of your fingers it took a turn. It wasn't just the smell that got me, it was the reaction my intuition gave me as well. I went from laughing and joking to RUN AND GET THE F**K OUT OF THERE! I admit it, I get spooked and the fight or flight kicks in but I can usually shake it off or I will run away a little bit and stop. Not this time. I ran out of that tunnel and was about to run the half mile to my car. If I was alone I would've but I stopped once I got outside and waited for them to come out.

I am deathly afraid of snakes and heights and whatever that was made those fears feel obsolete. That felt like true fear. Like the fear of all fears. I truly believe whatever that smell belonged to was the entity that tried to stop me from helping the spirits the last time I had gone with my cousin. If my intuition hadn't kicked in and I felt that pure rush of terror overtake my body I would've just thought someone had passed gas and made fart jokes. I did not want to be there any longer and that was the end of that trip for me.

As we were leaving to add the cherry on top of the ice cream, my wife who is amazing at receiving messages from spirits was texting me. She told me she could see a non-human entity following me not too far behind me. It was coming for me. I could feel it as well as she was seeing it. I could then see it too once I focused for a second. The closest way I can describe what we were seeing is to imagine Ghostface from the movie Scream. However, it had no legs or face, but the body looked like the costume Ghostface wears. There it was hovering towards me like a predator stalking an injured animal.

I started walking even faster, telling it that it had no permission to follow me, begging my guides to safely get me out of there. I just wanted to get to my car, use some sage, and get the hell out of there. I truly to my core believe this is the same entity or a similar entity to the one the other investigator wrote her book about and he wanted my soul for helping the others escape. A soul for a soul. This is why I have not gone back. I am terrified of whatever is or was waiting for me at those ruins.

I have not been back since that day. In fact I don't even like driving close to it. I did one night as I was heading to the SK Pierce mansion in Gardner, MA, from New York. My quickest route brought me a half mile away from the prison. As I got closer, objects in my car started acting up. My oldest kid had a Hulk RC car that was in my back seat. There were no batteries in the car or even the remote (I was using them for my ghost hunting gear) and yet the car started talking like it did when you drove it around. It would say "Hulk smash" and make his grunting noises and that's what it was somehow doing. Then my car radio started changing stations by itself once I fixated on the Hulk car. The thought of returning to these grounds are both terrifying and intriguing.

# CHAPTER 5:

## EVEN IN THE AFTERLIFE, FARTS ARE FUNNY?

Phew, now that we got that trip down memory lane over with let's go to a place that is not too much better history-wise but is not so scary revisiting. My first full swing at mixing Paranormal Investigation with Urban Exploring. We are going to one of the oldest institutions that served individuals with developmental issues in the Western Hemisphere of the United States. Walter E. Fernald State School, located right in Massachusetts. This institution was founded and opened in 1848 by Samuel Howe in Boston, MA going by the name the Experimental School for Teaching and Training Idiotic Children.

The school moved to its new permanent location of Waltham, MA between 1888 and1891.

In Waltham, the school development ended up expanding to 72 buildings across 196 acres of land. In its peak there were 2,500 people living at the campus; most of them were "feeble-minded" boys. It was during the tenure of the third superintendent, Walter E. Fernald (1859-1924), when the school started to be viewed as a model educational facility in the field of mental retardation. Doctors and politicians from all over the U.S. and the rest of the world would visit Fernald to study the experiments they were doing at the development. For example, Fernald created the first independent farm colony for the disabled, known as the Templeton Colony as well as early concepts of special education.

Another experiment that took place at Fernald was that of radioactive isotopes. These experiments were held by MIT Professor Robert S. Harris and one of the sponsors was Quaker Oats Company. They would feed students that were in the "Science Club" radioactive iron and calcium mixed with oatmeal and milk to study the absorption of iron and calcium. They got the students to join this "Science Club" by offering larger portions of food, parties, and even going to

Boston Red Sox games. There was a total of 57 students who ate the radioactive oatmeal and 17 that were given radioactive iron supplement shots. Radiation levels in their stool samples and blood levels served as dependent variables. Neither the parents nor the students who volunteered were ever given sufficient informed consent for the studies.

Walter was seen as an important figure in the eugenics movement. Advocating for the segregation of mentally disabled children from society and coining the term "Defective Delinquent." This referred to and described the children that were "criminally inclined mentally disabled children." Towards the end of his life he was second guessing many of his ideas and ended up fighting the segregation of mentally disabled children. Unfortunately it was too late as forced segregation and mass institutes had already been introduced to the American mainstream. Walter passed away in 1924, and the school was renamed in his honor in 1925.

The institution served such a large population of children with cognitive disabilities. This led to poor living conditions such as approximately 36 children living in and sleeping in a single dorm room. Due to the poor living conditions there are reports of both physical and sexual abuse. In the 1970s a class action suit *Ricci v. Okin* was filed against Fernald and other institutions for persons with intellectual disabilities to upgrade their living conditions. Fast forward to 2013, Fernald is still open but only 13 patients are still living there. One of which was a resident that was 84 years old and had been living at Fernald since the age of 19. All of its other patients by this time have been moved to private, community-based settings with better living conditions. Fernald ended up closing its doors in 2014, as its last patient was discharged Thursday, November 13$^{th}$.

Now, doesn't this place sound amazing? Choice of radioactive oatmeal for breakfast and sleeping with possibly 35 other individuals. Sounds like a blast to me. In all seriousness, I have been in those dorm rooms, and

I cannot wrap my head around and even think of how up to 36 people were shoved into those rooms. The rooms on average are about (give or take a foot or two) 15ft x 20ft. Those poor residents must have been shoved in there like a can of sardines. I forgot where I heard it, but someone had come across some tapes that were left behind from doing some exploring there and they watched the documented footage of them rewarding the "Science Club" by giving them McDonalds. Shout out to whomever was the one who found those videos and shared that story with me.

I have gone to Fernald three times (maybe four) total. Each trip was unforgettable. So, we will dive into each one. I have never done this location alone. I wish I had the guts too, but this is a location that had my nerves in overdrive every time with other people being there with me. I cannot even imagine what it would be like going one on one with this one. This was my first big exploration of a hospital/institution and I was excited. My mother-in-law had gotten me a book for Christmas of abandoned places in Massachusetts, and once I read about this location I knew I had to check it out for myself.

My first ever trip here had me hooked on this place. We had parked down the street by a playground and made our way to the development. We found an abandoned house on the main road which looked like it would've been housing for staff, or small private sessions for children (because I have seen pictures from the inside of this house looking building and it has a bunch of old stuffed animals and games inside) and cut down into the woods from there. Getting in was the easy part, getting out, not so much. It was early October, so we had some of Mother Nature's help still with the tall grass and some leaves on the trees to help keep us hidden. We made our way down what looked like a dirt road that headed right towards the church building of the institution. The front door of the church was wide open, so we decided to start there.

This church was so dark inside from it being boarded up that the spooky atmosphere kicked in almost instantly. This being our second big exploration and it being a new location we did want to walk around and check the place out quickly. It was our first time being in an abandoned and potentially haunted chapel after all. To be honest, I am not a religious man. I do not believe in Hell, Heaven, God, Satan, Demons, or Angels but I know churches and places of worship are supposed to be that of "light" and "good." Therefore, I was not expecting much or any interaction for bible readers and believers say that there are no spirts, that all spirits are demons. And if demons cannot enter sacred ground, sacred buildings, how would spirits be in here? I do not want to get into politics about "God" so I am not going into what I truly believe to the roots of my soul so I will stick to the spooky stuff. But I was not going to risk sneaking inside to not even give it a try.

We did just that. After getting the sightseeing over with like kids let loose at Disney Land, we got to business. I thought it would be a good idea to set up and try at the altar, almost like church was in session. I wanted to see who would be willing to come talk to us. I had set two cat balls on the lectern (podium) and stepped aside. As soon as I stepped down and went to walk away one of the balls started to light up. The floor was kind of hollow, so I thought maybe the vibrations of me walking had set it off.

The ball stopped lighting up so I started to stomp my foot as hard as I could, to the point I hurt my ankle and then jumped a few times to see if it was from me. I could see the ball make a slight wiggle, but it did not light up. This was one of the first times I had seen one go off with my own eyes, so I had to make sure and see

why it was going off. I then asked if someone had done that when I stopped stomping and jumping around and again it lit up. Seeing the interaction with the little light I quickly got out a Necrophonic to see who was here with us and willing to chat.

It was like opening the floodgates as soon as we got the Necrophonic running and opened up for conversation it was full speed and non-stop. You could tell there were many eager spirits that wanted to talk and be heard. We spent a good forty-five minutes, maybe longer. They kept mentioning demons, evil, Satan, the devil. This is my first time being in a church establishment, well at least when it comes to communicating with the other side.

All I knew at the time is these buildings are supposed to be holy beacons of God. If this is the case, then how could there be evil in it? It really had me questioning what they were really trying to tell us. Was it because of the place itself and the experiments they would do to the poor residents of the facility? As I was trying to dig into what was being said, trying to get them to talk more about the "evil" it sounded like some kind of heavy animal was running circles around us.

I could hear it on the floor by us, then the walls, then back over by us, then back on the walls surrounding us. Literally doing laps and each time it came by us it got closer. You could hear the weight behind it and the distinct sound of claws/nails scraping the floor as it ran a couple laps around us. This was the first time hearing anything like this, so I was rather intrigued. I was more curious than scared. There was something inside me though registering that whatever this was, it was not friendly and we needed to wrap it up and get out of there. Being new to this at the time, I never questioned those intuitive feelings and made sure to wrap it up and head on out of there.

From the church building we made our way down the street (yes, this facility has its own streets as that's how big it is) to a building that looked like a small schooling building. It had four floors; the basement, main floor, and second and third floors. The first, second, and third floors looked like little classrooms. We walked around a bit, exploring the building, feeling out the energy. It felt new but at the same time there was a familiar feeling, an energy I had felt over at the chapel building. As if someone or something took the offer to follow us around and chat with us.

This was my first time being in an abandoned establishment like this, so I was all about the sightseeing, walking from room to room. It was almost as though I could see the place as if it was still operational, as if a spirit was showing me. It was amazing to have that connection to open up to a new world. What I find funny, more on the ironic side, is that in school I hated history classes with a passion, and now I go place to place trying to dig up the past through spirits. To be fair most of the history teachers I had growing up had dry sandpaper like personalities. I did however love science and electronics classes growing up which is vital when exploring the spirit world as well. They all tie together.

After exploring a bit we made our way to the second floor by the main staircase, and I pulled out a Spirit Box and we set up a cat ball over by the stairs. As we were talking to them I felt the urge to ask if they had followed us from the church to see if I could get them to confirm what I was feeling. As I asked if they were following us from the church through the Spirit Box they said "Yes" and "Show them the light." As they said "Show them the light" the cat ball that was set up over by where my cousin was started lighting up. Seeing and hearing them mention a light and then making the cat ball go off was amazing to witness and had us both very excited about what was going on.

It was starting to get darker out, the sun was setting quickly. We wanted to try and explore and see as much as we could before it got too dark. Also, I do not like being in these locations after the sun sets because you need light more and I do not like chancing the light to give our whereabouts away. I am willing to take risks but in a strategic way. Like a plus sized, squishy ninja. We walked around trying to see what building to go into next; this place is massive and has so many to go into. I knew there was no way we were getting into each one to try and talk to the spirits.

After a quick lap and exploring of the grounds, seeing what was still accessible, we ended this trip in what looked like a giant cafeteria. It had almost identical setup to a school's cafeteria and cooking area except it looks as if it was made to hold a couple hundred people at a time versus a grades worth of students. We walked through where it looks like they would've all ate and headed to the back section where it looked like the meals were prepped for distribution. We set up a REM-pod, some cat balls, and got out a Spirit Box.

The whole trip prior to this moment was "wow!" "This is really amazing!" And this is where our trip went to "Oh my god, what the fuck is happening?" It is dark at this point, it was at least 7:30-8PM by the time we started in this area. There were puddles of water all around us, you could tell parts of the roof were missing and where water was getting in during storms. I don't know if because they say water is a conduit for spirits and we were opening up to communication to the spirits, but it went from nice casual conversations to holy shit, what did we get ourselves into?

As we were talking to them through the Spirit Box, from one of the walk-in freezers it sounded like someone banging on the walls. I went and looked; no one was in there. It was just me and my cousin. Feeling a little uneasy we kept talking to them but now we were in alert mode, trying to watch the equipment we had spaced out and yet watch from all around us. Behind my cousin along the wall there was a ladder adhered to the wall that led into what looked like an air duct system.

We had a moment when I stopped the Spirit Box and it sounded like someone walked up the ladder and started crawling into the vents. Again, no one was there, just us and I had my vision on the ladder as this happened. We started to focus on the ladder and try to see what we were hearing. Just then the REM-pod that was behind me started to go off taking our attention off of the ladder. At this point, I am starting to feel a little freaked out, I will be honest. I hid it very well at the moment, but I was starting to get scared.

Remember how I made sure to mention there were water puddles on the floor from the leaks? Well, there was a reason I made sure to point those out because they are about to really come into play. Someone was about to creep us both out to the point we began questioning our sanity. The ladder/vent incident simmered down as well as the REM-pod and chatter on Spirit Box. So, I was trying to entice them to talk to us some more thinking they got bored with us and moved on. I was wrong, so wrong.

As we were shifting our focus on the cat balls seeing if they would light them up for us like in the church and that schooling building we heard what sounded like someone with bare feet running through the puddles on the floor. We both looked at each other as if we were mentally asking each other, "did that really just happen?" Once we both realized that we both heard it we started geeking out. We caught our composure but as we did, in another puddle on the floor, it happened again. At this point, I am beyond good. Between it being a little later and spending about ten hours there, and now all this freaky crap happening I was ready to call it quits.

Even as we were wrapping up getting ready to head out, the running through the puddles doing laps around us continued a few more times. Needless to say, this was one of the freakiest encounters I have ever had at an abandoned location in which someone else was with me. Alone, I have had scarier but that is a different location and a different chapter, so make sure to keep reading. Anyways, we parted ways with this location and headed home.

I wish I could say getting out was as easy as getting in, but I would be lying. We got lost. So lost. First, we walked past the section of woods in which we had entered from. I knew the woods looked a little different, but it was dark and hard to tell. We got up the hill partially and there were a bunch of thorn bushes which we had not seen on the way in, so that is what gave away the error of our exit. We then back tracked towards the middle of the field. It took close to a good twenty minutes of me flashing my light around to find the trail we had entered from.

This moment led to my cousin bringing rope to tie around trees during the next visit. Sorry, I know it's not a creepy moment, but this was a funny ditzy moment that I had to share. We knew after this trip and all we had witnessed a return visit had to happen. We knew we had to go back and see other buildings and try and see if more spirits would be willing to talk. We did just that.

It was getting closer to Halloween of 2020 and all the "pay to play" locations were booked up and we wanted somewhere epic to investigate and put on YouTube. So, what do we do? We go and visit the old administration building of Metropolitan State Hospital (which is basically neighbors with Fernald) and Fernald. This trip was with my cousin, a fellow paranormal enthusiast that is really good with the Spirt Box (and has some really nice custom ones), and a female who was good at her mediumship and receiving messages from spirit. This was an amazing trip and experience, regardless of what happened between me and the others.

We made our way through the trail my cousin and myself had used last time. We started with the church again. With how amazing it was last time I wanted to see if we could have a similar interaction again. Plus, we took some cool Halloween like pictures of ourselves for fun. After we were done goofing around we got ready to see who was willing to chat with us. As we were setting up my cousin was walking around just checking the church out and getting some filler footage for the video.

This part cracks me up and never grows old. Farts, especially with good timing can be hilarious. Apparently even in the afterlife that humor carries over. Because we didn't know this at the time but as I was reviewing the footage to see what I could use for the video I found something I will never forget. My cousin walks into another room and as he is walking around recording there is what sounds like a fart noise, followed by a hilarious EVP. I do not know if the fart was my cousin letting one loose because he was off alone or if it was a ghost fart, but either way, you clearly hear the fart noise. There is an EVP saying, "Fart so no one can smell it," sounds of someone trying to push out a fart, and then the fart noise. It is then followed by an EVP saying, "good fart." That was the most innocent thing they said in this church and once I heard this I was in tears laughing and will never forget such a capture.

We were set up over by the altar of the church. We had a REM-pod set up on it, and we were using a modified Spirit Box that the other enthusiast had built. It was modified to cut out the radio stations better, making it easier to hear what spirits are trying to tell you over the white noise/static that is in between each station. We could most definitely hear them better. One spirit proceeded to tell us that he has a big c**k, and then when the enthusiast asked if they were sinners they proceeded to say that they want to be. For a church, these spirits were getting a little freaky.

But the moment we witnessed in person that stands out the most from the church section was the very intelligent REM-pod interaction. A standard REM-pod has four colored lights and the closer you get to the antenna and more you touch it will trigger the lights a certain way. Basically from further away to closer/right on top of it. Well the REM-pod was going off and I wanted to see if they could make certain lights of the device light up, almost like Simon says. I would say please make the blue light go off, and they would manipulate the REM-pod just right until the blue light went off, same thing with red. Only one they had trouble with was yellow because it is one of the middle colors. Nonetheless it was really amazing to watch them manipulate the device trying to make just the yellow light go off. It really showed they were there with us, listening to us, interacting with us.

Because we had stopped at two other places before we made our way to Fernald we did not spend too much time in the church. We wanted to cover as much ground as we could and try to get some more evidence from other buildings. So, after the few good interactions we got from the Spirit Box and REM-pod we packed it up and ventured off to explore more of Fernald. We visited a few other buildings for the remainder of the time we were on the property. The second building we made our way into looked like one of the main buildings.

This is how I know the rooms were small and said I couldn't imagine that many people trying to bunk up in one room. My cousin and I found ourselves in one of the further bedrooms where we had found an old-looking blanket. Upon investigating the blanket we found a good amount of blood soaked into it. As we did the Spirit Box I was running mentioned blood. I asked if the blood belonged to them. As I did the lights on the EMF reader I was using started to flicker. I asked if that was their way of confirming what I was asking, again they light up. To be on the safe side I asked them to light up the EMF reader one more time if they were confirming all my questions. A third time, they triggered the device for us.

I tried asking several times for their name, to try and help in any way which I could, but we never got a name. We mostly explored this building, though that one corner bedroom was the most we investigated in it. We made our way into what looked like another building for practicing religion. This was not set up like a Church, more like a normal building with religious symbols all over it. I did not recognize the symbols and therefore was not even going to make an assumption of what religious practice it was used for.

Anyways, the reason I remember this building so well is the vastly strange experience we had in the basement. I don't know why I was so drawn to the basement, but I really wanted to check it out. We get to the end of the basement where all the boilers are. I felt like I was living a Nightmare on Elm St movie being in that area. Some shady stuff could go on down there and no one would even know. The woman that was with us was picking up the spirit of a child down there. This is where it gets really strange.

As she was picking up the spirit of the child, she would say what she was picking up from him. To see if we could validate what she was receiving for messages from him I would ask him to the light up the EMF reader for yes, and leave it alone for no. It was working and as we were really trying to piece the story together of the child (he was starting to tell us about a faculty member that would take him and others down into the basement for abuse) she picked up on another spirit, the spirit of someone who resembled a janitor. It was the faculty member the child was telling us about. He was trying to silence the spirit of the boy. Stop him from telling us things.

We got a Spirit Box out, trying to confront the janitor/faculty about what the child was saying. And he clearly did not want to talk about the subject at hand. He was telling us to stop asking and would hear him say "stop talking" which sounded like we were picking up him telling the child to be quiet. The child was getting scared of the faculty member, I told him he could stay with us, and kept encouraging him to talk and not be scared. After I could tell the faculty member was not going to cooperate with us, I told him he had no power and was to leave the child and other spirits of children alone. She said not only did the presence of the faculty member vanish almost instantly but that of the child as well.

Between what was going on with everything, the Spirit Box, EMF reader, the medium, especially the atmosphere of the place as this was all happening, this was one of the strangest experiences I have ever had; at least back then. I seem to find myself in these situations a lot when investigating. Whenever I get a spirit trying to tell their story, another spirit tries to silence them. Then I confront the bully spirit and either the bully stops, gets more confrontational and the spirit that was trying to talk disappears leaving the bully to win. This has actually gotten me scratched several times, I don't care though. I hate bullies, both physical and spiritual.

We packed it up, explored a couple other buildings, spending a few more hours here before calling it a trip. We explored a big hospital building (I wish I was brave enough at the time to wonder off alone, that place had immense energy, and I know if I had wondered off something would have scared the shit out of me), and even explored the library building. This was the last one we did before heading home. No matter where we went after those first three buildings, nothing even came close to how intense they were. I will never forget that trip. Oh, and we didn't get lost trying to make our way out like the first trip.

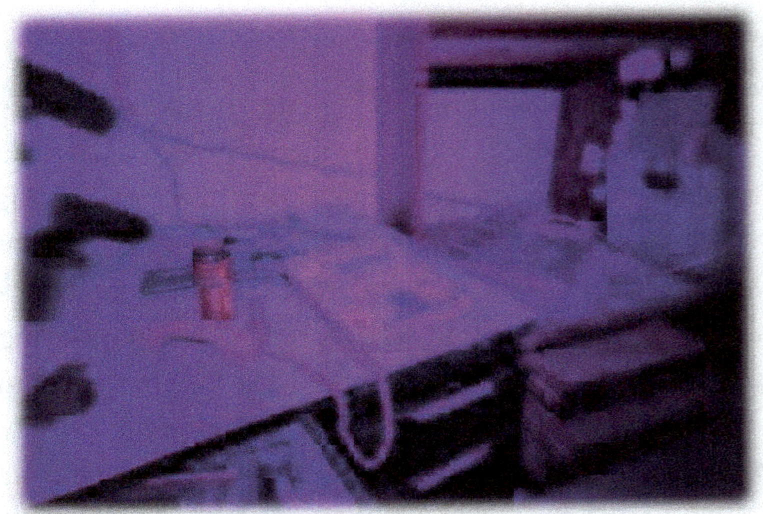

This leaves us with the last trip I made there. I am sort of itching to try it again but at the same time I kind of want to leave this one in the past. There was another YouTube channel doing a charity event for Christmas, so I volunteered with my cousin and I to partake. We recorded a video just for this event, never even threw it on my channel. I thought it would be a cool idea to go to Fernald and try to help spread Christmas cheer to the spirits still there. Let them have somewhat of a Christmas again. The old auditorium building was still there and accessible, so I wanted to go there and play some Christmas songs for them.

We did just that. We made our way to Fernald with some Christmas flair, Christmas spirit and most of all ready to spread some Christmas joy. I dressed like Santa, my cousin an elf. I even used white hairspray to color my beard. We wanted to give the spirits a good old-fashioned Christmas concert. We slowly made our way to the auditorium. It was the last building I wanted to do. You know, save the best for last. I had no idea how crazy the detour to the auditorium would be and what we were about to witness. We first explored another smaller housing building. Nothing too eccentric happened here though. Typical investigation, somewhat quiet, not too much activity. We went through this one first because this was the first year the town had set up one of those drive-through Christmas light displays and we had to work our way around it to get to the auditorium.

However, this next building that we entered was where the trip gets strange, inexplicably strange. The next building we crossed paths with to get to the auditorium was the main administration building. That's right, the building where it all starts and ends with the patients. This was my first time doing a building like this and I was stoked. There was no clear path on how to get in this one, however, I was NOT leaving without getting through. It was dark now already so finding an entrance point at the time was more on the difficult side. But after heavy searching and much dedication, we found it; our way in.

I may or may not have helped the influence of the entrance and I am not that type, however there was a call from that building so strongly that I needed to know why I was being called in. I felt like a dog scratching at the door because I know my owner is on the other side, needing my help. In fact, what happened to us in this building is so messed up that I am pretty sure I did not use it for the charity video. I used some of the footage, but if I am remembering this correctly there was one part that is so messed up I did not use that footage.

As we were investigating, SpiritTalker started to mention things about a shooting, bullets, and blood. We were confused as to why we were getting these messages, but as soon as we turned our flashlights on low and started looking around, it all made sense. In the wall in several different areas there were bullet sized holes. Some barely penetrating the wall, some going in deep. But no blood, so what did it all mean? As we looked around some more, we found it, BLOOD! Along the other wall on the side of the room, closest to the door was a red trail, which to us looked like blood. It started on one side and made its way down the wall towards the main door of the room and stopped on the back side of the door because I closed the door following the trail and that's where it ended?

Was there really a shooting there? I tried to Google for answers but could not find anything. Did the spirits think there was a shooting and trying to share with us what they thought happened? Or was there really a shooting that is not documented that the spirits witnessed and told us about? I am not sure, but this moment is one of the freakiest I have ever witnessed. I know I may get spooked; I may scream and run, but having spirits share something so obscene is a bit nerve-wracking. I just asked follow-up questions to what they were telling us but had no such luck.

To this day I still question what they were saying to us. If it was all legit. If it all really happened. After not getting anywhere with the follow-up questions we made our way over to the auditorium building for the Christmas special for the spirits. We got inside and set some equipment around the room. A REM-pod on the stage with some motion activated balls.

On the main floor we set up a few motion activated balls as well. I wanted to see if blaring some Christmas tunes and singing along trying to bring the spirit up for them would show results. As much as I was hoping the tunes and cheer would work, it did not. In fact the most activity or action we got while in this building was security or patrol doing a round of checkups in which we had to hide low until they passed.

Even though we did not get any communication through the Spirit Box of what we were trying to do for them, I hope the spirits enjoyed the show. Hopefully they got to enjoy some of the Christmas spirit and joy.

# CHAPTER SIX:

## SEVEN TEETH

Now, this is going to be a shorter chapter because I have only been to this building twice, and in which only one of the trips was inside. Even though it was only one trip, it was fun and unforgettable and worth the share. As I said in the opening, I do not want any locations to go to waste. There is only one building left of this establishment and it is the main administration building. Because I quickly mentioned it in the last chapter, I want to share this location next. We are going to Metropolitan State School. This was one of the locations that helped inspire the American Horror Story: Asylum season.

Metropolitan State Hospital's founding originally began in 1900 when legislation was passed by the state. However, because of trying to find an area big enough to house the hospital didn't come easily and on the quicker side, it did not get its roots until 1926. The site was constructed in the greater part of Waltham, parts of Lexington, and parts of Belmont, MA. October of 1930 is when the hospital formally opened even though construction would carry on until 1935.

In its peak it housed 2000 patients. Its doors would remain open until 1992 when the facility was closed during a deinstitutionalization movement. The state (Massachusetts) closed down most of the state's mental hospitals and Metropolitan was one of them. The patients were placed in smaller settings and housing. There is not too much history to find about this location online. However, one of the most bone chilling events that happened here was the murder of Anne Davee, who was a patient at the time by a fellow patient named of Melvin Wilson.

In August of 1978 Anne Marie Davee (age 36) would go missing. About two months later the search was taken more seriously. By this time potential evidence was destroyed and leads were not followed.

Even the evidence of finding her clothing, and a hatchet were ignored and overlooked. Six months after her disappearance (February 1979) the hospital tried saying that Anne was discharged. It would be eight months later that Melvin Wilson (Age: late 50's) who was now in Bridgewater Hospital would be found for the murder of Anne. He was at the time of Anne's disappearance at Metropolitan with her. He was able to bring the police to the few holes (3 to 4 holes) he had buried her in for her bodied was dismembered. Melvin even kept seven of Anne's teeth, which is part of how he was caught.

He was sent back to Bridgewater Hospital for observation before being held at trial in court for the death of Anne Davee. Anne was in and out of mental hospitals in Massachusetts and Maine for 18 years before Melvin, who was in hospitals for forty years, would take her life in a gruesome manner.

The main hospital itself may be hard to find some eerie stories, however, if you were to research the Gaebler Children's Center you can read some stories of patients and the awful lives they lived while being there. Even a creepy story from "a nurse who worked there." The Gaebler Children's center was the building used for children to young adolescence. It opened in 1955 near the grounds of Metropolitan and was named after the second superintendent, William Gaebler. The Gaebler building would remain open until 1992 when the Department of Mental Health (DMH) would shut it down because they deemed it as no longer being able to serve the needs of the children it housed. I am good friends with someone who went to Gaebler and got to witness this place firsthand. They wrote a short passage for this chapter which I will share now before diving into how creepy this place was on the inside:

Looking back, it's hard to be angry about my placement here. I'm not by any means saying I enjoyed it, but it was the mid-1980s, and that was about the only option given to my family. Things were not like they are now, with wonderful hands placed on me. After an incident that resulted in my expulsion from public school, I spent four years going to school here.

One of the first things I need to point out is that a lot of these kids were wards of the state, and they simply did not have enough foster homes—or homes that could take on troubled kids. It was really a mixed bag of children from across the Boston Metro area. I was lucky to live in the same town, and my parents did not fear having me live at home. I got to sleep in my own bed each night, unlike so many others.

The station wagon I had for a school bus would pick me up early and return me every evening. There were two buildings in the Gaebler Children's Center: the big building "Up the Hill" and a smaller building "Down the Hill." Gaebler was secluded from the rest of Metropolitan State by a wooded area. I honestly had no idea it was a whole hospital campus until I was an adult. I just thought it was a school for bad kids. My family was told I would be down the hill in the smaller school with the students, but I spent time in both buildings year-round.

There was a very different feeling to each building. Down the hill felt a lot like a mainstream school and definitely looked it.

Up the hill was completely different. We would ride in a van up the long drive to the imposing building that stood there. There was a main hall with beautiful woodwork and an inviting atmosphere. At the end of that main hall stood a locked steel door. Once through that door, you were at the mercy of the staff. Some staff were great, others, not so much.

I learned my first lesson here very quickly, and it was not a good one. I learned that if I wanted to survive, I needed to quickly become someone that was not to be messed with. It was a lesson nobody should have to learn, much less before hitting double digits in age. I adapted quickly and made the right friends—well, right for keeping me safer against the other aggressive children. The staff was a completely different story, and they took a hands-on approach to behavior modification. No friend was able to help out with that.

Do you remember what I said at the beginning about how I dealt with having hands on me? Yeah, this was a long, hard road I was about to go down. At nine, I was not a big kid, and having five staff members on me at once was overwhelming. At the first sign of agitation, they would hands-on try to remove you from a room. I would react and quickly learned what the floor polish tasted like. I know how far up my back my arms can bend without actually dislocating my shoulders. At nine, I knew the weight of a knee in my back from a full-grown man. I knew more than I should have.

It truly was the madhouse it sounds like. It was worse up the hill in the big building. Here, you would be locked in, ward to ward, and hall to hall. The windows had wire in them, the doors were made of metal, and the chairs and other furniture were hard and uninviting. I also got to know from the other students what it was like to live there. They were medicated at night to keep them calm. There was talk about abuse at night, but I will not share details as they are not firsthand stories. Remember, I got to go home at night.

However, my time here was not good, but it made me a stronger person in the end—not thanks to the school, but in spite of it. I became a parent who needed to find proper placement for my boys, one of whom is on the autism spectrum. My life lesson was thrust back in my face 30 years after leaving when I went to tour potential schools. I remember most vividly at McLean being told that there were still remnants of the tunnel system that used to link them to Metropolitan State Hospital. While McLean has a beautiful school, I couldn't do that to myself.

I find going back to these kinds of locations to be so cathartic. I feel for the kids who had it worse than me and especially for the ones who never made it out. It has allowed me to reconnect with those emotions and to begin healing from them. I have a fondness for the spirits left behind in these schools and hospitals because I know what life was like in part. I think if you take one thing away from this story, it's this:

> If you go for a visit to a school or hospital to investigate the paranormal, don't assume all the children were disabled. Don't assume anything at all! Let them show you who they are, and they might surprise you. They are spirits from the human realm and need love and respect—especially the ones still trapped with the ex-employees who are still lingering as well.

Thank you so much for sharing this experience of yours about this location. It is not every day that I know someone who attended one of these locations that I have been to. Now, let's dive into what the main administration building was like on the inside. Again, this is the only building still standing from this establishment. And honestly, I didn't know if we were getting in or not. This was just a visit before Fernald. In fact, we ordered some pizza and ate it right on the front steps. Prior to stuffing our faces, we walked around the area, trying to get a feel for the place. Even the grounds had a dreadful feeling to them.

After our little snack. We made our way inside the admin building. The front door was wide open, so we did not let this trip go to waste. Once you cleared the doorway and got out towards the main hall, the energy of the place shifted so much that all four of us felt it and confirmed it. It was not due to the darkness because we were still in a well-lit area, but it was more like we had a crowd all around us, surrounding us. Because we hadn't planned on this location and we were not sure if it was going to be accessible or not, we got a bit carried away and started running around scoping the place out in excitement. There was a basement floor, main floor (the one we entered from), second floor, and an attic floor. The attic floor had a ladder that went out to the roof, and the view was amazing from here. After running around like kids given a bunch of caffeine for the first time, I wanted to see if we could get any of the spirits to talk to us.

Since we had all just finished exploring the second floor which had an eerie vibe to it, we started off there. We started off in a back corner room with a Spirit Box. We were getting all kinds of chatter. It was almost as if we had opened the floodgate to communicate. For confirmation of us having communication with intelligent spirits, I usually ask the color of my shirt, or hat, something I can point to and try to get them to say it over the Spirit Box. I try to stay away from asking how many fingers I am holding up because numbers are common with Spirit Box. But the enthusiast we were with took it up a notch and pointed to some graffiti on the wall and asked the spirits to say what he was pointing to on the wall, this was after asking the spirits to repeat some words he was saying.

Within a minute a spirit responded with "black cock" for he was pointing at a graffiti drawing of a giant black penis. I know, people have such amazing artistic skills, yet these locations sadly always get the short end of the stick by getting penises drawn all over them. It's always a penis or some racist bullshit. People are so ignorant. When the spirit responded though with that answer, we couldn't help but burst out in laughter. We didn't see that one coming at all. We poked around shortly upstairs and sadly the best interaction we had

was that of the graffiti scrotum on the wall. Don't get me wrong, that crap was hilarious, but I did want to be able to share some stories of those still around other than penis jokes. We had some other interaction and chatter, but nothing like what we had just happen, so we decided to make our way to the basement to try some more.

As we made our way down the stairs and entered the basement area it was as if we had entered a whole new area. The atmosphere of what was down there was on a completely different level than what we had just walked through. It felt more depressing, angry, and you could feel the darkness surrounding the darkness that was created by the lack of lighting. The basement was trashed badly. Honestly, I'm not sure how safe it was to be on this lower floor. But we tried it anyways.

We wandered down the hall and headed into a room that was on the right side of us and tried an EVP session. This was the first one we tried in this building, and it paid off. Usually spirits mention wanting help, needing help, feeling like they are trapped wherever they are. But whoever we made contact with during this moment was not and they made it very clear. I always like asking if there are any spirits that need help or would like to leave where they are and at this moment I asked some questions along those lines. I asked if they needed help leaving. If they were stuck there and when we did a playback of the recording there was a very firm male voice saying "no." I always get blown away when catching direct responses, this is some of my favorite evidence. And no matter how many times I catch the voices of spirits both residual and intelligent I am overwhelmed with excitement and thankful to have captured that moment. The only part of this moment that caught me off guard is why anyone would want to remain at this hospital. It didn't sound like a pleasant spirit either by the tone of the voice and how he had said no either.

We did three EVP sessions in this room before making our exit to a smaller room that was across the hall from where we just were. In this room I wanted to go on the newer side with investigating and used an application on my phone that is made for spiritual communication, Necrophonic. Phones have glass, crystals, batteries, and radio waves from phone towers. All forms of energy that spirits can manipulate, so yes, I do believe some applications do work on phones, especially when you get a very coherent response as we are about to get in this room.

Remember in the quick history breakdown, the sad story of Anne Davee being brutally murdered and her killer Melvin keeping seven of her teeth? Well, I wanted to try to see if we can make contact with her or get confirmation about what had happened. And I would get my answers. I asked who was in the basement with us and it said "Anne." That was a good start, we were making connection with Anne. Then I was trying to see if we could find out how Melvin had murdered her and it then through Necrophonic it said, “Broke my neck.” The only part that has me somewhat perplexed was the teeth. I asked how many teeth were kept after she was murdered and it said, “get it right” and then what sounded like “five.” If this is the case and Melvin really only kept five of her teeth, did the reports get it wrong? Or did he keep trophies from another victim who was never discovered? Or was this just another spirit messing with us, throwing us off track? We shall never know.

Even though I have only visited the remains of this hospital two times, and been inside the one time to investigate, it left an everlasting impression that will forever stay with me.

# CHAPTER SEVEN:

## TAP, TAP, TAP AT MY FEET

This next location is probably one of the creepiest places I have ever been in alone. Yet, I did it more than once. You can say I have issues. I push the spiritual boundaries too much sometimes. I did it once and it was one of the scariest experiences I have ever had. Yet, I pushed myself to go a couple of more times alone. I did do a trip with a friend and fellow explorer which wasn't as creepy, but I did catch one of the best captures I have ever gotten on video, and honestly, it will probably never happen again. I mean, I hope I get more like that capture (spoiler alert, I have), but it is a one in a million capture. And if it does end up being the only one, it was an epic capture, and I will always be grateful for it. I caught a shadow figure on video. But we will visit that moment later.

We are going for a visit to Lakeville State Sanatorium, which today it goes by Lakeville Hospital or Lakeville State Hospital. It originally opened its doors in 1910 as Lakeville State Sanatorium, part of the states 20th century public health response to the tuberculosis epidemic. It practiced the cure of the disease with heliotherapy. This is the use of sunlight and sun exposure. Lakeville was considered an ideal location for this because of the size of the hospital and how well it was isolated from the public.

From 1936 and on the sanatorium started allowing admission of patients with poliomyelitis (infantile paralysis), spastic paralysis, and "crippled children," those with orthopaedical-type conditions. By the 1950's and decline of tuberculosis in Massachusetts, the sanatorium really needed to shift its focus on the types of patients it would admit. The sanatorium would then start taking in patients of "crippling conditions" such as arthritis and muscular dystrophy, and similar diseases.

In 1954 Lakeville would start providing care of aging person and in 1957 would start taking in those with chronic diseases. In 1963 the name would formally be changed from Lakeville State Sanatorium to Lakeville Hospital. Fast forward to 1991 under the Executive Order of Governor William Weld a special commission for the study of Consolidation of State Facilities aimed to reduce costs and close deteriorating physical plants. This led to the closure of Lakeville Hospital and in February of 1992 it ceased operations.

Though the hospital was not opened long, it ended up offering a wide array of those it would try to help. Now what is left of the hospital is slated for demolition for commercial and residential use. Demolition has already started and it is becoming more and more a distant memory of what it once was and getting harder to sneak in for a spooky visit, or those who just love to explore old buildings that are no longer being used. To the point it is basically very dangerous. As tempted as I am to go for one last hello, I think it is safer to just write for you, the experiences I have had with the few trips I have done.

If I recall correctly, I think I have made it a point to visit this old hospital at least five times. However, there are three visits which stand out the most. The ones I really, really want to share. That being said, let's start with the first trip I ever took. This was a solo trip and one of the scariest moments I have ever had. I have done my fair share of screaming, I admit it. In fact, I willingly share the videos on my socials. It is hilarious and I own those moments. However, this moment was so creepy that it froze me in my tracks. To the point I thought I was capital fucked.

There used to be a door on the back side of the building that was ground level and busted wide open. It had heavy plastic covering it. So right off the bat it already had the horror movie vibes, but I didn't think I was going to be walking into one. I made my way in; place is somewhat lit from the windows and broken doors but had its dark patches. So, I am thinking to myself, this isn't so bad. I can do this. I could feel the energy of the place though and part of me wanted to say nope and leave as soon as I walked in. But I was very eager to check the place out for I knew there wasn't much time left for the place. And I know that a place that is explorable one day may not be the next, so I did not want to miss the opportunity.

I took a deep breath, psyched myself up mentally and made my way around. I was walking on nerves, but I managed to pull out some ITC apps and see who was still around and if someone was willing to chat. And just like a lot of locations that don't have crazy people like me sneaking in to chat, it opened up a floodgate of many willing to talk. It was very overwhelming with how much was coming through. It was very hard to keep up with what they were trying to share. I didn't hear this with my own ears, only when doing the playback from the trip but I caught a woman screaming at the top of her lungs. If I had heard that while walking through the dark, decrepit halls, I may have shit myself and left my pants on the floor and drove home in my underwear.

I spent about a good half hour or so walking around half of the first floor. I didn't want to go too far because towards the other end you could hear the generator to the trailer where the security guards would stage up. I did make it into a room that almost looked like a theater, if that is what it was, it kind of makes me happy because it showed they tried to hopefully keep the spirits of the residents up with shows. And if it wasn't a theater room, I would not be able to guess what it was. It had a stage, so I will stick with my guess. I stood in the doorway of that room though, but didn't make it far in. Something inside me was telling me not to go in, something was hiding in the dark. And some of the stuff coming through the ITC apps was not too pleasant, so needless to say, I did not stay there long. After my departure from there, I really pushed myself by going down to the ground floor/basement.

As I made my way down the stairs, my adrenaline really started to course through my veins. For every step I took the darkness seemed to surround me faster and the vibes were getting heavier. I got down the stairs and made my way through the door. I shut my light off just to see what I had got myself into and that did not last long, for the second that light went off, I felt as if I had been surrounded and something wanted to charge at me. I couldn't even see my hand in front of my face. I turned my light back on and made my way down the hallway.

As I made my way down the hallway I saw a giant room to my left that had some natural light illuminating it and wanted a break from the darkness, so I darted over into it. This room was massive and I could see all kinds of equipment still in it. Looked like sterilization machines. I walked to the other end of the room and looked out the door and again was just surrounded by darkness, so I decided to play it safe and walk back into the sterilization room. As I was walking back to the other end that I had entered from and set up my gear to do some investigation, that's when I had the most bone chilling experience I have ever had.

I was about halfway when I heard the sound of bare feet slapping the tile floor that surrounded me. I could hear someone running at me full speed, but there was no one there! Right as the sound got next to me the slapping sound of the bare feet came to a sudden halt and as I stood there trying to grasp what was happening, someone let out a very loud and distinct sigh right into my left ear. I was frozen completely, shocked and too afraid to take another step. After a couple of seconds passed, probably about 5-10 seconds, but it felt so much longer than that and since nothing else happened, I psyched myself back up and made my way to the other side of the room and pulled out some ITC equipment to try and make contact with whoever had just scared the hell out of me.

However, just like upstairs it was like I had opened a flood gate, and everyone was trying to talk all at once, and it became more overwhelming and frustrating than coherent. No matter how hard I tried to steer the conversation it did not work. As much as I love exploring these places to try and give them a voice, it gets a bit frustrating when it feels like you are walking in circles. So, I thanked them for talking to me, even though a lot of the times they would say things that made no sense to me, to us that are still physically here,

I feel like just offering an ear can be helpful. I grabbed my stuff and slowly made my exit as I took the scenery in. This trip will FOREVER live in my head rent free.

This next trip is a real doozie! I had a friend who is really into Urbex and the paranormal meet me here for this one. If you watch Nuke's Top 5 on YouTube, or the television show Fright Club, you may already know the trip we are going to talk about. Or maybe you have come across it on my own socials. I had this moment blasted everywhere! If not, you may want to save this part for when it is dark and spooky because this one, well this one is freaky as hell and honestly, one of the most mind-blowing moments that I not only witnessed with my own eyes but caught on video!

We walked around for a bit on the main floor when you first walk in. But now that I had someone with me and thought the basement would be less terrifying after my last encounter here, I really wanted to see if we could find the morgue room. I had seen pictures of it, so I knew it was still there. I was wrong about it being less creepy though. I had no idea or could have ever imagined what was going to come next. After exploring the basement floor for a bit, making a lot of wrong turns and guessing, we found the morgue/body room.

After surveying the morgue for a hot minute, I had this crazy idea to lay in one of the mortuary racks myself, and I did. I was just really being drawn to one of them and I had to find out why. My friend had stayed on the opposite side of the preparation table or autopsy table, (not sure which one it is but was definitely used to examine the bodies and drain the fluids) and got ready with her voice recorder for an EVP session.

As I was laying there I swear I could see orbs all around me. Orbs can vary in shape and sizes. Most common ones you see look like little white or yellow balls moving through the air. Very similar looking to dust on night vision cameras, that is why so many people mistake dust for orbs. But when you can see little balls of light moving yourself, well, you most likely saw a spirit zipping by. It was starting to feel a little heavy on the rack, a little scary as well, but I wanted to push myself, so I continued to lay on the rack.

This is where this trip really starts to get wild. As I am laying on the rack I could hear someone tapping on the rollers down by my feet. Quickly after I started to hear the tapping, I began to feel the tapping. At this point I am really starting to feel a little freaked out. But I kept on pushing it. Then the noises started to sound like they were coming from the rack above mine. So, I not only look up, I pan my phone to try and see if I could see anything, but no, nothing. Then the tapping started down by my feet again, so I slowly pan my camera down to look towards my feet to see what was going on. There was so much happening all at once, my mind was starting to race.

I have my camera now looking at my feet, but I was more so using it for the flashlight for I when I was really getting creeped out, I had turned it on. I was not watching anything from my phone, just trying to capture the moments as they happened. This put my phone in my line of sight and as I tap my toes together (I have a very hard time sitting still) I watched with my own eyes what looked like the shadow of a child crawling up from my rack to the top rack on my left. Like, literally watched it with my own eyes. I was completely shocked. I could see the light of my friend's light staying perfectly still as she was doing a playback of her voice recording. Even knowing that it was not her I had seen, I called out to her asking if she was moving around.

She confirmed that she was not moving, and I was so in shock of what I had seen that I doubtfully asked her again if she was moving. Again, same response. She was just standing there listening to her voice recording. I find this part kind of funny, where most people would have freaked out and got the hell out of there, I just continued to nonchalantly lay there as if nothing happened. Not much longer after that, she mentioned that it was starting to feel really creepy in the room, so I got off the rack to join her.

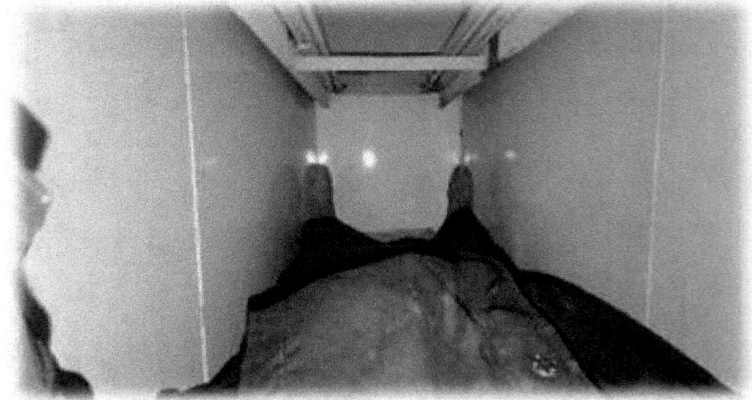

After exiting the rack and busting her chops saying that the room wasn't creepy, that she wasn't the one having someone tap down at her feet. We then ran Necrophonic for a little bit before switching over to some traditional Spirit Box. After running them for a bit I could feel and tell the vibes in the morgue room were different, less heavy and not really worth poking around at anymore and decided it was a good place to end that trip and pack it up. Of course, we had to do some sightseeing on the way out. It paid off too; we got to see the room they used for the sun therapy sessions during its time as a tuberculosis hospital. As well as finding and seeing some of the therapy baths they used, before they were removed for the demolition.

Anytime someone asks me, especially skeptics, to prove that ghosts are real, I always show that clip of catching the child sized spirit hop from my rack to the upper left one next to me. Even some of the most skeptical people that I have shown that video to are left speechless after. It is hands down one of my best captures, not my favorite paranormal moment, not even in my top five, but it is definitely one of the most compelling. A moment I will always remember.

Capturing that spirit on video was not enough for me, I wanted, no I NEEDED more! So, what do I do? I go back, but this time, alone. I now know how messed up and how scary this location is, but something inside me wanted the full effect of that scary basement alone. That is exactly what I did, I headed back there, but only with me, myself, and I. Knowing exactly where the morgue was played out in my favor, for once I arrived I knew exactly where to make a run for.

Now, I know that "lightning doesn't strike in the same place twice" but there is always that little bit of hope in me when returning to locations that I can capture something similar or better than the last trip. So, I head right to the room and stage some REM-pods on the racks and get ready for a session. I contemplated laying on the rack again, but as I did, I envisioned a spirit being an asshole and closing it fully shut entrapping me in it. Not having anyone with me to bail me out in case that actually happened, I played it safe and walked around in the room as I tried to communicate with any spirits that were around instead. As I was doing so, I had an odd sensation to walk around more of the basement floor and explore a part I had not done yet, this isn't normal for me, for I like the Urbex aspect, but I go for the ghost stuff.

I didn't fight the feeling and made my way towards the front of the building on the basement floor. It started to get light around me because there were ground level windows that were smashed open. This allowed me to get some really cool photos and explore a part I had not seen before without being scared, for it felt more calming. And that was where I made my mistake. As soon as I got too comfortable and started to enjoy the sightseeing more than talking to the dead, it went south.

Not only was I starting to feel like I was being followed, but I was also hearing the noises as if someone else was there walking around. I went from chill and relaxed, to creeped the fuck out. I even hid in a room peaking the doorways, as if that was going to work for hiding from a spirit, hahahaha. I went from taking pictures to recording video, because well, let's face it, if something super messed up was about to happen, I was not letting that moment not get captured. This wasn't a quick moment either, it went on for a couple of minutes. I got to the point where I decided I should do a quick little fat shuffle out of there. But instead of leaving like a logical person, I headed right back to the morgue room.

Now, do not ask me my logic to this madness, for even I don't know what the hell I was thinking. Knowing me, I figured if it is starting to get scary as hell, ride it out but in a creepier space for the views. Not the smartest of ideas, but hey, it worked out in my favor. It seemed to calm down shortly after going back in the morgue room. So, I was like alright, let's get some cool pictures in here and then get the heck out of there. The lights I usually carry on me have three settings. Clear/White light, low red light, and purple/UV light (the ones hunters will use to track blood).

I got my flashlight set to red and take some shots. I also have the light from my phone on because I am shooting video still. I shut the light to my phone off to make it super creepy. As I am taking the last few pictures, someone bangs on the counter right behind me that I was leaning against. Sounding just like a quick and rapid knock. It knocked three times. It freaked me out so badly that it almost made me feel more at ease. I know that sounds very contradicting but in some weird way, I was like oh, there's my big scare of the trip, no point of running out now. I did freeze for a moment, but then I carried on with trying to get some cool yet creepy photos.

After getting my photos, I was somewhat scared but still wanted to explore. I knew that this was probably my last trip here. It was getting harder to get into, the building was getting in rougher shape, and they were starting to watch it (security) even more. So, I decided to make the rest of the trip a casual walk around, getting some more video. To say goodbye to this location. To close out this chapter of my adventures. That was almost five years ago now, from the time of that trip to the time of me writing this.

The buildings are still there, as of now. It is in really rough shape and watched even more by security and police. My TikTok algorithm keeps showing me all the newer explorers and their moments from there. Part of me is tempted to go back to chat one last time, to take some pictures one last time. Spring is around the corner. Only fate can decide if I face this behemoth one more time, or if I just let it lay to rest. To enjoy the memories, I have from there and move on to the next.

# CHAPTER 8:

## A NIGHTMARE AT ELMCREST

This next location will be the one to end this particular journey. Don't you worry, there will be more. However, I want to try and keep each book that I write about ghost hunting mixed with Urbex to be, I don't want to say shorter, but I want each location to shine, to really be absorbed by the reader. Not to have too many locations in one book, I feel like that will take away from each location, and I don't want that. Plus, the ones I have saved for book two, I am not done with them. There will be more trips to them.

This location I sadly only got to do one time. By the time I had heard about it, it was already slated for demo and there was not much time left for its hollow shell to stand. I was actually on the way there for a second trip with a friend, I thought it would be a cool location to record a Halloween episode for YouTube, but as we were about to head there, a fire had broken out. We ended up having to detour to another location.

I find it kind of sad that this location we are about to visit doesn't get talked about nearly enough—Elmcrest Psychiatric Hospital in Portland, Connecticut. Unlike the massive institutions people usually picture, Elmcrest is tucked away on a quiet stretch of land, made up of old estate homes that were never meant to be locked from the inside. It opened in the 1940s and spent decades treating children and adults with mental health needs. From the outside, it looked calm, almost inviting, but as time went on and ownership changed hands, the atmosphere inside began to shift. By the 1990s, cracks were showing—staffing issues, procedural problems, and a growing sense that the place was barely holding together.

That brings us to 1997, the year Elmcrest stopped being just another psychiatric hospital and became something heavier. It was purchased by Saint Francis Hospital, which brought its new name St. Francis Care

Behavioral Health. In 1998, An eleven-year-old boy named Andrew McClain was admitted for treatment. During a behavioral episode, staff restrained him face-down on the floor, applying pressure meant to control him. Instead, it killed him. The cause was ruled traumatic asphyxia, officially labeled an accident. No charges were filed, no crime acknowledged. Policies were changed quietly afterward, but the damage was already done. From that point on, Elmcrest carried a reputation that never really left, no matter how carefully reports were worded.

Not long after, the hospital began its slow shutdown. By the early 2000s, patients were transferred elsewhere, and Elmcrest's doors closed for good. The buildings were left behind to rot—windows smashed, roofs collapsing, hallways open to the elements. Years later, fires tore through parts of the abandoned campus, as if the place was erasing itself piece by piece. Locals stopped seeing it as a former hospital and started seeing it as something to avoid, especially after dark.

Today, all of Elmcrest has been demolished or redeveloped. But like most places with this kind of history, the land doesn't forget so easily. Official records say there was no murder, no wrongdoing—just an accident. But history lessons aren't only about what's written down. Sometimes they're about what gets explained away, sealed up, and left behind in buildings that were never meant to hold that much silence.

I don't know if it is not talked about as much because compared to most institutions around the area, it had a shorter lifespan, or because maybe not as much tragedy happened here as what did in other locations similar in nature. But I feel like this location needs more awareness, and preserved history of it in books, or videos for all to see.

Hopefully, those who have posted videos of here start getting more visibility. Doesn't even have to be my video. Or maybe you learn a little something about it reading this book. Even if this helps the memory of poor little Andrew live on. It will mean something. But it can't die with the buildings, the story must continue on.

Which brings me to the next part of this chapter. The exploration of it, or what little I got to do before another great exploring location was wiped off the map forever. I absolutely loved getting to walk the grounds. The only downside was, where I had made my way through, there was so much overgrown grass that I think I was more worried about snakes and ticks than squatters. I felt like I was in The Lost World of Jurassic Park. Growing up, I watched the first two movies religiously so, I sort of felt like I was living my childhood favorite movies in a weird way. Obviously, there was no giant ass dinosaurs trying to eat me or stalk me. But I was definitely being followed.

I made my way through the tall grass and into the first building. It was not a large building but fairly sized. It looked like it had about five or so classrooms in it. I could still see all the lesson boards up on the wall. I took a few pictures of it and video but did not try to establish connection with any spirits yet. I waited until I got into the upper floors before trying anything. I entered the upper floor, doing my initial sweep. I like to do a sweep sometimes to look for any potential dangers before getting too comfortable and talking to spirits.

What I found wild is I have been into quite a few psychiatric hospitals "asylums" and never come across a padded room; until now. It was tiny as heck too. I would say maybe 5ft by 5ft the most. Not giving much space to whomever was placed in there at all. Just picturing the inhumane ways they were treated is heartbreaking. After doing my initial safety sweep I was walking back to the main corridor while doing more of the Urbex sightseeing.

I got into a small little office area, and I heard what sounded like a door squeak. Now, I know I am alone, I checked all the rooms on that floor, so to be honest I got pretty creeped out. I instantly went into stealth mode and was trying to listen for any footsteps or signs of maybe someone who got in there too. I stopped talking normally, went to whispering (I was filming for YouTube) and turned the brightness down on my light. Nothing. And then the vibes, the energy started to instantly shift. I knew I was not alone. I knew it wasn't a physical person.

I knew it was time to try and make connection. So, I headed back to the main corridor area. Because if shit went south, I wanted a fast exit, the exit was about 50ft from where I decided to stage up. Also, it was well lit, lots of natural light coming through the windows. Even though I know the light doesn't mean anything, it somewhat puts my mind at ease. Because if a spirit is going to mess with you, they will mess with you regardless if it is light out or dark out. Darkness just adds to the spookiness of videos for the views, but in actuality it doesn't mean shit.

At this time I was heavily using SpiritTalker, I mean I still do. But this was when it was newer on the marketplace and I was loving all the results I was getting with it at other locations, I will swear by this app and how scary accurate it is. So, I booted it up alongside the GhostTube SLS app. This is an app that will work on any phone or iPad that has Lidar technology in the camera. If the phone or iPad does not have Lidar in it, I hate to break your heart, but it is not legit and you are seeing ghosts on it that are really not there, basically, it is false mapping on you. Even with Lidar the SLS is iffy and can false map a lot. That is why I personally do not use it a lot and only get excited about stick figures on the camera if I am getting EVPs at the same time, intelligent Spirit Box responses, or other equipment going off that can validate the silly stick figure.

This is where this trip starts to get really freaky. Like not just here and now, but the rest of the trip. Shortly after turning on Spirit Talker, I started getting responses about a sore neck, broken which led me to be curious as to why I was getting those responses. Something inside of me told me these few phrases and key words were significant. Which typically, I am not usually to have those strong feelings, so I knew I had to do some research. I had not done any research prior to my visit. All I knew was it was a psychiatric hospital and it was not open that long. I like to go to locations blind sometimes and see what I can find out about the place by spirit communication.

That's when I found the story about poor little Andrew and what had happened to him. I knew right there and then why those words were so significant, why I had such a strong urge to do some research on the location and any history of neck trauma. I made contact

with Andrew, and I wanted to help share his story, so I made sure I added what had tragically happened to him in my video, and now in this book. I hope his spirit finds peace. I hope sharing his story helps. Back to the rest of the trip now.

To be honest, I was not expecting to try and go full swing investigating here. I had left most of my gear in my car because I was on the way to another location and this one was a random, spur of the moment, off the beaten path trip. I am glad I did the detour, for like I said in the opening, I had planned to come back with a buddy, but a fire prevented that. So, had I not done this random visit, I probably would have never got to see it before it was gone.

After leaving the main building I made my way into the next closest one to me that was accessible. It looked like an arts and crafts building. The second floor had long counters with a few sinks in them, what you would see in an art room, or even a science room. I did not investigate in here, hell, I didn't even last long in here. I made my way to the second floor and as I was taking in the views, it sounded like someone was following me. I started to feel as if someone was trying to sneak up on me. I felt surrounded.

Every time I would turn my back towards the stairs, I had used to get to the second floor, the sounds of being followed got louder, the presence got stronger. I found myself freezing like a deer in headlights, waiting for the jump-scare. I was living a real-life horror movie. My mind's eye did not like what I was seeing. Something felt heavy, like it wanted me. Again, the place is well lit, like I said, darkness doesn't mean shit. If a spirit is going to fuck with you, they are going to do it in the light as much as the dark. I didn't run out of the building, part of me wanted to wait it out, see what was going to happen. The logical side of me was saying to get the hell out. So, I went the logical route and made my way out.

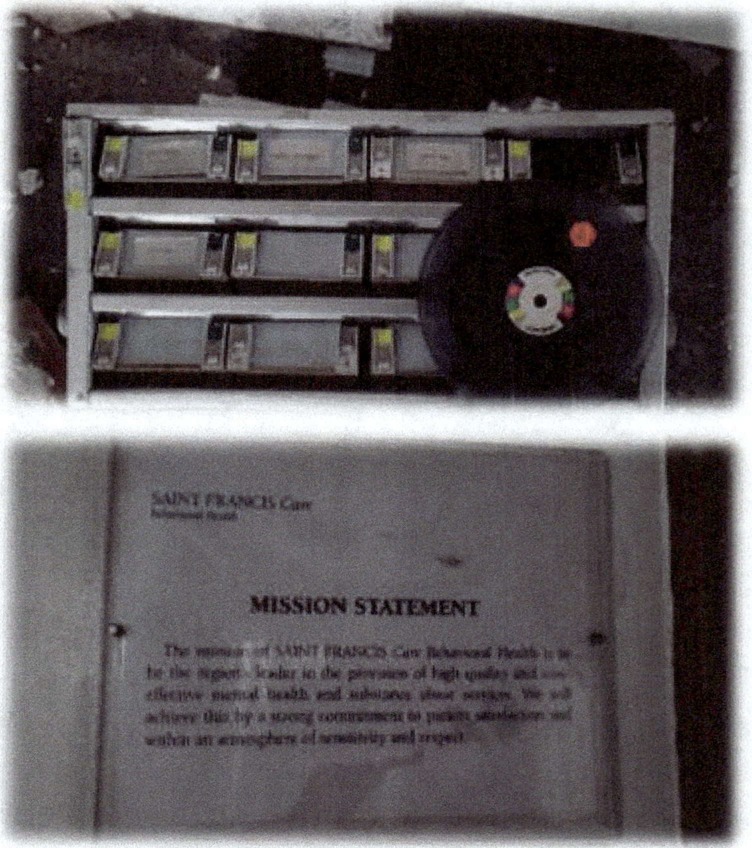


Every building I entered, as soon as I started feeling safe, then that heaviness started following me. I knew I was being followed. So, I would walk with Spirit

Talker, but I didn't sit in any one spot long. In fact, I turned the trip more into an Urbex visit and started concentrating more on the exploration of it and taking some pictures and videos. I knew this place was worth investigating, but not alone. After a few hours of this back and forth of being followed by something heavier and scarier feeling, I played it safe and recorded an outro for my YouTube video and made my exit.

It sucks that I never got to make it back with more equipment and really try to make an established connection with whatever or whoever was haunting these grounds, but it is something I cannot change, and I am just thankful I got to see it at least once and have an experience I will never forget. I am thankful this trip led me to learn about Andrew and try to share his story even more to those who may have never heard it. I know I had not until visiting Elm crest and getting those responses on Spirit Talker. It is a trip that will forever leave me wondering what if.

# CLOSING

I really hope you enjoyed this haunted and disturbing journey. I say disturbing, not for all the creepy paranormal moments and encounters, but because of how we as humans treat one another. The way some of these places used to operate and some still continue to operate to this day. This may be the first of the series, but it definitely won't be the last.

Again, I ***do not*** condone or recommend the actions I took to get these stories and or photographs. If you do, have some damn respect. I cannot tell you how many videos and photographs I cannot use or share due to inappropriate graffiti. Spray painting and tagging locations is not only ignorant, but it looks like shit. No one will ever respect you. Also, racism just wrong in general, and you look like you have the mentality of a child when leaving such distasteful markings.

There is a saying in Urbex that everyone who does it really needs to learn to live by. I know I can be guilty myself of taking items from places. I know I have good intentions of what I do with them, but I have been living by this rule for a while now. No longer do I take anything from the places that I visit. Unless it is a dirt sample or a brick. That saying is:

***Take nothing but photos, leave nothing but footprints.***

# Syllabus

All of the information provided during the historical part of each chapter was information that was accessible on Google. Straight forward information you can find online by looking each location up. The only part that won't be found is how I told you about the mafia working with the prison guards of Rutland Prison Camp. That was from a source from someone they knew that worked there.

I did not do any excessive research and provided the spark note history of each location. More of a spark note history lesson to help paint a picture of where we were and to help you envision the place better. So, there is no traditional syllabus page. I did not want to find myself in endless rabbit holes of darkness that can be found of each location doing excessive digging. If you would like to do so, be my guest. But be warned, you may not like what you find.

www.ingramcontent.com/pod-product-compliance
Lightning Source LLC
La Vergne TN
LVHW010607110826
845149LV00003B/812
* 9 7 9 8 9 9 4 6 0 1 0 4 4 *